WITHOUT PREJUDICE

A Donny Weston – Abby Marshall Thriller

By

David O'Neil

W & B Publishers
USA

Without Prejudice © 2014. All rights reserved by David O'Neil.

W & B Publishers

For information:
W & B Publishers
Post Office Box 193
Colfax, NC 27235
www.a-argusbooks.com

ISBN: 978-0-6920243-8-6
ISBN: 0-6920243-8-7

Book Cover designed by Dubya
Printed in the United States of America

Chapter One...Off the cuff

The finish on the hull looked good to Abby Marshall as she wiped a paint-spattered hand across her forehead. She was not aware that there was now a white mark there, to accompany the smudge of blue which had come from the broom handle Donny Weston had been using for applying the anti-fouling.

Swallow was looking good in her old age. As a personal task undertaken when Donny's parents had given them the boat during their last year at Brunel University, they were in the final stages of the complete overhaul they had promised themselves at the time. It had taken longer than anticipated, because various events had interfered before they could get started.

Now she would take the water once more, five days hence.

The yard foreman had promised the crane would drop her in at high tide. With the engine tuned and the masts and rigging ready for a light crane to drop into place as soon as she was afloat, they would have plenty of time to move her to a deep-water mooring to complete the setting up for her voyage south.

"I like the make-up." Donny grinned at Abby as she added to the white marks on her face. "The blue and white is a step away from the pallor from too much swotting and too little open air."

The easy relationship between the two young people was the result of several years' friendship and considerable personal danger shared since they first met at the age of sixteen. Then they had been at high-school. Now coming up to twenty-one, five turbulent years later, they were engaged and both poised to embark on their new career to become barristers.

Abby touched her face gingerly. "They are the badges of honest labour, earned through hard work. I note the absence of any such decoration on your unsullied countenance." She flicked a few spots onto his face, the white paint decorating him to her satisfaction. He grimaced and clapped his hand to his eyes.

"Oh, no. Has it gone into your eye?"

She rushed over to see the damage. Donny grabbed her and held her close. rubbing his spattered cheek against hers. "No. I just wanted to share the moment with you. That's all." He burst out laughing at her smeared cheek.

Abby smiled ruefully. "Okay. You got me. Can we pack up now? I've painted everything that is nailed down."

Donny stood back and looked at the graceful hull, gleaming in her new paint; white hull and blue anti-foul. "She'll do!" He said. "We can put the remaining gear on board now. There will only be the fresh food to load when we set out."

***

There was wind and sunshine when they left Christchurch harbour, Abby at the wheel, the ketch heeling under the pressure of the plain sails. Below, Donny was checking the contents of the concealed locker behind the bench seat-back. The old towel on the table was covered with the assembly of weapons they now had available. Walther PPKs, Glocks, a Browning .45—five automatics in all; an Armalite .375, and a Winchester bored for .22 Hornet cartridges. The two H&K Mk3 smgs were separately racked with spare magazines in slip-on harnesses beside them.

He returned the weapons to their place and closed the locker door, calling to Abby through the open hatch, "You ready for coffee yet?"

"I'm always ready. It's about time the workers on this bucket got some attention."

Ignoring the slur on their beloved craft, Donny put the coffee on. As he poked his head out of the cabin he looked at the sky and decided that the weather was not too unkind. The sea was moving but the waves were not bad for the time of year. *Swallow* was cruising easily with little sign of the pounding that the short stiff seas the Channel often created, though they had not yet reached the more open waters of Biscay.

They anticipated staying at La Rochelle for two days at least before sailing on to their eventual destination in Malta, where the boat would remain until next summer.

***

Inverbervie, Scotland

The sun was low in the autumn sky. Long shadows cast black silhouettes on the ground from the row of trees between the man and the horizon, stretching for miles out over the water.

There was no sign of the ship, and it crossed his mind that being late seemed to be a way of life in this particular part on the world. The *Aurora* was a research ship en route to the Arctic-circle. He had been told there would be a place for him if he was in Inverbervie when they called.

With a sigh the fair haired man with the intense blue eyes shouldered his pack and made his way down to the harbour office.

The Harbour Master was a slim, dapper, ex-Naval officer, complete with a trim beard and moustache combination.

As Tom Hardy made his way through the door of the office, the harbour master, Captain Henry MacNeil, RN retired, looked up at him. "It looks as if you are really out of luck. The *Aurora* has engine trouble, she will not arrive today, possibly not even tomorrow. If you really need to get away today, you'll need to try one of the yachts. I hear that *Stroller* is planning to move today. Perhaps Peter Speight will give you a lift." The smile on his face gave the lie to the suggestion.

Tom grinned ruefully. "I think I'll give that suggestion a miss. Is anyone else on the move?"

The Captain straightened up. "Will Pleasance is showing signs of getting under way again."

Tom looked at him sharply, "Will Pleasance?"

"He owns *Speedwell*, the schooner moored on the end of the quay." The Captain sounded serious and Tom was a little surprised at the suggestion. In the three weeks he had been here in Inverbervie the schooner had not shown any sign of moving. Still, he had not spent all that time here at the harbour.

"I thought it was permanent," he said, a little uncertainly.

The Captain said dryly, "I believe the hull is tight and the rigging is new. I can assure you that Will Pleasance is no myth. He is well-known in this area as a sailing man of wide experience. He has reported that he will be leaving for Le Treport and La Rochelle. I'm pretty sure he could use an experienced hand to help out on the trip. I'll call him if you'd like?"

Tom shrugged. "Why not? France is good at this time of year."

The Captain picked up the receiver and called the *Speedwell* on the radio phone. When the call was answered he said, "Will, I have found you a crew. Shall I send him along?"

The voice at the other end said something that Tom did not hear. The Captain laughed and said, "Not this one. He even sounds like a Scot. His name is Tom Hardy." He put the phone down and turned to Tom. "Right, lad. On your way. He expects to sail in just over one hour. So don't hang about."

Tom picked up his pack and swung it onto his back. He held out his hand, "Thanks, Skipper. I appreciate the help."

"Have a good voyage and watch out for those bloody tankers. They take three miles to slow down." He grinned and turned back to his desk.

Handing a sheet of paper to Tom, he said, "Give this to the old bugger. It's as up to date as it can be."

Tom looked at the paper. It was the latest weather report.

He waved and departed down the steps to the quay outside. Turning to seaward, he headed for the two tall masts of the schooner at the far end, beyond the rows of boats filling the marina along the inner harbour wall.

On his way he noticed the sleek length of the *Stroller* just starting to move out of her berth. Nadine Speight was coiling the stern line while her father, Peter, handled the helm.

Tom had to concede that Peter could handle the 65-foot power cruiser, as he skilfully threaded his way between the pontoons to the harbour entrance.

Nadine spotted him as she finished with the rope. She lifted her hand and waved. He waved back. For some reason he felt relieved that she was sailing away in a different direction to his own.

At the end of the quay the schooner, *Speedwell,* sat alongside, rocking as the lift of swell created by the passing power boat pushed her against the fenders protecting her hull from the jetty wall. Tom looked down at her lines visible below him in the evening light. He approved the graceful sweep of her deck planking running for a full 80 feet. Her bowsprit projected beyond the upswept bow. Looking aloft he noted that the rig was a modified Bermudan, which would make her a lot handier for a small crew, especially with the winches installed for sail handling. There was a man standing beside the deck house forward of the main mast.

As he stood, the man hailed him. "Would you be Tom Hardy?"

"I would," Tom replied. "Will Pleasance, I presume?"

"Come aboard. We'll be casting off shortly."

Tom swung down the iron ladder that clinging to the quay wall at that point, and stepped onto the deck still moving under his feet.

He walked aft to meet the big man, who was in turn walking toward him.

Tom was perhaps two inches taller, but Will was more muscular. Greying hair stuck out from under a Breton hat.

The pair looked at each other each, weighing the other up.

Will put out his hand, as Tom shook it. Both decided that the other looked okay.

"Call me Will or Skipper, whatever you like. We'll call you Tom, if that's alright."

"That's fine. Where do I stow my gear?"

Will turned and called out. "Lotte! On deck, please."

A tousle-haired blond head appeared through the hatch of the deckhouse. "You don't have to shout so loud, granddad." The head was followed by a body, all of five foot six with a trim waist and a bare midriff. The cut-off jeans reached her calves. Lotte turned to see what the fuss was about and stopped suddenly, looking at Tom in surprise.

He returned her look with interest; *about twenty,* he thought, *and pretty with it.*

The blue eyes weighed him up warily. She decided she quite liked what they saw. "Introduce me to you friend." She said in an even tone.

"Is your Gran there?" Will said.

"She is storing the provisions in the cuddy." Looking at Tom, she held out her hand. "I'm Lotte Compton, granddaughter of this old pirate. I currently seem to be dogsbody on this ship. And you are?"

"Tom Hardy, hoping to be spare hand on this ship."

"When you two have finished holding hands, I would like to get a few words in." Will interjected drily. Both of the younger people hastily dropped the other's hand at this.

Turning to Tom, Will asked, "Have you sailed before?"

"Yes. I have done some sailing."

"Nothing of this size, I suppose?"

Tom said, "Actually, yes. I have a sailing master's ticket, from St Johns, Newfoundland. I was Mate of a Grand Bank's schooner, doing fisheries research last year.

Will grinned. "You're pulling my leg!"

Tom reached into the side pocket of his pack and drew out his papers. He handed them to Will without a word.

Lotte looked on with interest, as Will perused the documents.

While this was going on another head appeared at the hatch. "Charlotte, take these, please." A tray appeared with mugs on it, the steam making ripped patterns as the wind caught it.

Lotte took the tray and handed Tom a mug. She put the tray on the deckhouse roof as the slender figure of her grandmother appeared. "You must be Tom, the man that Captain 'thingamy' said he was sending down. I'm Mary Pleasance, the skipper's wife. How do you do."

"Tom Hardy, Mrs. Pleasance. I'm pleased to meet you."

"Have you finished reading those papers, Will? Your tea will get cold."

Will looked up. "Get your gear below, Tom. Missus' will show you where. Lotte, let loose the foresail and number one jib. We'll motor off, then set the other sails." To Tom he said, "Back on deck as soon as you like. We have plenty to do."

Below, Tom found he had a cabin to himself. He dumped his pack on the bed and hauled out his deck shoes and a pair of jeans. He changed, stripping off his shirt and pulling on a sweatshirt with a picture of a schooner on the back with the slogan, 'The best place for your savings, Grand Banks.

On deck he joined Lotte in letting loose the roller-reefed foresail. Mary was hauling in the fenders as the *Speedwell* pulled away from the quayside under the power of the Perkins diesel.

Once clear of the land and into Bervie Bay, Lotte and Tom winched in and sheeted home the two forward sails.

Will set the winch running to raise the mainsail. Mary started a second winch for the mizzen. Tom and Lotte stretched out the big mainsail and set it. Then, having set the mizzen, proceeded to trim each sail under instruction of Will, now very much the Skipper.

The weather was neither good nor bad. Away to the north the powerboat driven by Peter Speight could just be made out, riding a white cushion of churned water.

***

The schooner heeled in a most pleasing way Tom thought, as he sat with a hand on the wheel waiting for Will to return. The glow of the navigation lights warmed the encroaching night. The ship had Satnav, but Will made it a habit to check his navigation with sextant and stopwatch, as he had been taught when a midshipman in the Royal Navy.

For Tom, although he thought it a waste of time in the circumstances, he approved of the discipline. After all, if the power goes, so does the navigation.

He touched the wheel to port to avoid getting too close to the oil rig, lit up like Christmas tree ahead.

The log was reeling off a speed of ten knots. So, with all sail drawing well, the fresh breeze was working its magic and ship was demonstrating its clean hull and fine lines. Unlike the Grand Banks schooner he had sailed on, the *Speedwell* was built with a teak hull on oak frames, she was tight and dry. The pine planking of the American schooner had been losing integrity, the timber no longer as clean and tight as it once was. Though the hull had been beautifully drawn and the sail plan ideal, the aging timbers worked and she was well past her best. The *Speedwell's* hull though nearly 40 years old, was still as good as ever.

All this passed through Tom's mind as he, sat just enjoying being there. When Lotte appeared carrying a mug of hot soup and a plate of corn beef sandwiches, his day was made.

"Dig in, Mate. I've got the helm," Lotte said with a smile. She sat beside him, taking the wheel while he discovered just how hungry he was.

Lotte sat quietly at the wheel while Tom ate.

"What brought you to us?" She was curious.

"I had been ashore too long. I thought it was time to move on," Tom said quietly. "I was waiting for a research ship going to the Arctic Circle. I expected to sail with her, but she was already two days late with engine trouble. The possibility was she may take another two days to get there. Since I had already given up my digs, I thought I would see if anyone else was moving. And here I am."

"Not girl trouble, then?" Lotte looked at him sideways, a little line of tension showing as she made the suggestion.

Tom smiled, "No. Not girl trouble. Just what I said, itchy feet."

Lotte sat quiet for a while so Tom spoke. "No boyfriend waiting anxiously for you back home?"

"God, no. Anyway this is my home."

"Ah!" Tom said.

"Ah? What does that mean?" Lotte sat up, causing the wheel to move.

"Watch the course," Tom said. "It meant nothing. It was just 'ah'!"

"I saw you wave at Nadine Speight as they left the harbour on her father's boat. Do you know her well?"

"I've bumped into her once or twice, at the odd party in town. Why? Do you know her?"

"We were at school together a few years ago." Lotte did not sound pleased.

Tom recognised the edge in Lotte's voice. He turned and examined the compass, letting the silence build.

Eventually, she broke the silence. "Sorry. She was a bully at school. So I have never liked her."

"I beg your pardon!" He looked at her blankly. "Who are you talking about?"

"Nadine 'bloody' Speight. Who else do you think?"

"Ah!" Tom said once more.

"There you go again. 'Ah'!" Lotte said, sounding annoyed.

"Hold it!" Tom said firmly. "What is this about? Do you want to be my girlfriend, or something?"

"What? What do you mean?" Lotte blustered.

"Is that what all this is about? Are you looking for a boyfriend? Is that clear enough?"

"Why would you think that? I hardly know you." Confused, she looked at him.

"I asked first." Tom said firmly. He thought it might just bring her up short.

Despite being taken aback by his question, she thought about it as she studied the man sitting beside her. Her gaze was steady. For a moment she hesitated.

He could tell she was thinking hard.

Finally, she said, "Ok. Yes. I think I do."

It was his turn to be surprised. "You hardly know me. You said so yourself!"

"I'm getting to know you better all the time. I think you'll make a suitable boyfriend for me. Since we have Gran and Granddad to chaperone me while we get to know each other better, I'm willing to take the risk. Thank you for asking me. And once again, yes. I will be pleased to accept your offer." She swiftly leaned forward, kissed him firmly on the lips, and slipped her arms round his neck, holding him close for a breathless few moments.

"There, sealed with a kiss." She moved, turning to sit back in the curve of his arm, leaning against him companionably.

Tom sat without moving, making no effort to extricate himself. Lotte felt comfortable in his arms and he found he enjoyed the feel of the trim body pressed close to his. On impulse he turned his head and looked at her. She turned to see what he was doing. He tipped her chin up and kissed her gently on the lips. "A deal is a deal," he said quietly. "Though perhaps we should keep it to ourselves just now. Your grandparents may not understand."

Still looking up at him, she smiled. "You are probably right." She pulled his head down again, kissing him lightly once more. Then she sat up and moved over to the other side of the cockpit.

He sighed with relief, hearing the sounds of movement from below. Will poked his head out. "Are you two all right up there?"

"Couldn't be better, granddad," Lotte answered. "Hang on. Here are the dishes." She passed the sandwich plate and mug, and took the two glasses of red wine handed to her in return.

She turned to Tom and passed him a glass. In the light from the opened cabin door he noticed that she was blushing. His eyebrow rose in enquiry.

As she sat, Lotte giggled. "I just wondered what grand dad would have said had he looked out a little sooner."

Below deck Will turned to Mary. He shook his head and said, "I'm not sure who did what to whom?"

"What are you talking about?" Mary was preparing food for the late supper.

"She was grilling him about girlfriends. He said he didn't have one. She said, 'What about the bitch, Nadine?' did he know her? He said, 'Yes'. He had met her. She said, 'Nadine was a bully'. So he got clever and asked her if she wanted to be his girlfriend. I presume it was to stop her quizzing him about girlfriends."

"That makes sense!" Mary contributed.

"She said, 'But we don't know each other.' Did he want her as his girlfriend?

He said he asked first.

So she said 'yes.' She did want to be his girlfriend."

"So? Now what happens?"

"So he kissed her and she kissed him and they decided to keep quiet about it so we don't get upset."

"I had the feeling he was a sensible lad. So that's all right then." Mary said, "It's about time Lotte joined the human race."

Will looked at her warily. "You don't worry about it then?"

Mary smiled at him indulgently, ticked off her fingers. "One! Remember, Lotte is over twenty. Most girls have had several boyfriends by her age. Two! Tom had impressed me as level headed. After all he's what, twenty-eight, so he has been around a little, and I think she could do much worse. Three! She needs someone other than two old fogies, and since we are all in the same boat, what's the harm in it?"

Will looked at her fondly, stepped over and kissed her. "How I managed before I met you, I will never know."

Chapter two...the voyage

Will relieved Tom at 2200 hours, and Lotte came down into the cabin with Tom. Since Will had already eaten, Mary put food out for both the young people and went to her cabin, leaving them to finish their supper together.

They said 'goodnight' and went to their own bunks. Despite her attitude when she had spoken to Will, Mary was relieved, and was able to get to sleep after all.

Lotte sat the early watch from 0400, and Mary took over at 0800.

It all made sense and all four fell rapidly into the routine established that first night together.

The course was southward down the coast of Scotland and then England to the departure point at Ramsgate, where they called in to get fresh vegetables and milk before setting course for Le Treport, standing at the mouth of the river Bresle on the English Channel.

After checking in with the French harbour master, they entered with the tide, and tied up at the pontoon. Will arranged to refuel and top up with water while they were there. Then, saying he had some business to attend to, he changed into blazer and slacks, donned a tie and his best Breton cap, and disappeared for the rest of the day.

Tom spent most of the day checking the rigging for chafes, and the metalwork for rust. In the evening they dined at the Restaurant le Matelote, without Will, who had not returned by then.

Mary showed no sign of worry on Will's behalf, so the others were not concerned. Tom enjoyed the company, happy for the chance to get to know them both a little better.

He had realised that Will had been a Naval Officer retiring early five years ago. He had no need to buy a house, having inherited his parent's place overlooking the Solent when they had died while he was still serving. The house had been rented out ever since. On retirement, he had found the *Speedwell,* half converted from her former commercial state to her current use. The owner had run out of money and time at the right moment, and Will had been able to buy the boat at a price he could afford. He had replaced the engine with the current version when the dockyard at Rosyth had been holding an auction of unwanted gear. The conversion kit to Bermuda rig came from the same source, complete with main and mizzen masts. The sails were purpose-designed and cut. They were the single, most expensive items on the refit list.

The reconstructed interior had been almost done already. The final touches were going to be undertaken by Will himself.

"But!" Mary confided, "Though the enthusiasm was there, the skill was not. I was able to recruit the local technical college woodworking course to undertake the work, as a project for their City and Guilds. I am happy to say that the lecturer for the course was an old friend of my father's, it suited his book to have a joinery task for the course to round out their skills. It's just as well Lotte had not joined us by then. I think the distraction might have been too much for the workforce."

Lotte blushed. "Why do you say things like that? You make me sound like a glamour girl and I'm nothing like that."

Mary looked at Tom and he looked at her. Both were aware that Lotte had no real idea of how others saw her.

Tom said, "The workmanship is very well done. The ship is a credit to you both. By the way, what is our program for the next few days? Will we be staying here for long?"

Mary looked thoughtful. "Would it matter? I'm not quite sure why Will wanted to come here. I presumed it was one of his contacts from his Naval career. For that reason I am not too concerned at his absence at the moment."

Lotte left the table to go and watch a big gin-palace of a yacht negotiating the channel.

Tom took the opportunity to speak privately to Mary. "I thought if we were going to be here for a day or so, it might be possible to take Lotte off to Paris to see the sights? That is, if she would like to go/ Perhaps, if time allows, we could take in a little of the night life, though that would mean we would either have to find a hotel, or arrive back very late here. I could hire a car for the trip, or we could take the train?"

Mary smiled at him. "Have you discussed it with Lotte?"

"Have you discussed what with Lotte?" The girl herself said, as she rejoined them at the table.

Tom told her what he had suggested to Mary. "I thought since we were here, if we had time, you might enjoy the chance."

Lotte looked at Mary, "What do?..."

Mary held her hands up. "Don't ask me. You are a grown-up woman. It is time you started making your own decisions."

Lotte looked at them both in turn. Then she said. "Yes. I would like to go. But I don't really have anything to wear!"

Mary smiled, "I think that will be easily put right. You have a summer skirt and blouse, and your nice shoes which I know are low-heeled. But then you will have Paris. Your credit card has plenty of leeway. If you don't go mad you can expand your wardrobe quite easily without losing too much time. If you stay in a hotel you can dump your spare clothing and stay out late. There that's the problem solved. Enjoy!"

Lotte looked at Tom in question.

Tom smiled and shrugged his shoulders. "Why not? You are my girlfriend after all."

Lotte looked at Mary as she heard Tom's words.

Mary didn't turn a hair. "So, as long as nothing has changed since the first night, there should not be a problem."

"But how did you know?" she asked her grandmother.

"Your grandfather heard you two talking together." Mary said. "I approve, if it makes any difference. I think you are both sensible."

Lotte looked astonished. This was becoming surreal as far as she was concerned. Just a few days ago she had been the youngster, no real friends, enjoying life with her grandparents, no real responsibilities. Now somehow she had acquired a boyfriend and had passed into adulthood, and was calmly discussing sharing a hotel room with a man she had only met yesterday.

She looked up at Tom. He smiled at her. It was alright. As soon as she met his eyes she knew everything would be fine.

She looked round at her grandmother, smiled and said, "Is there anything I can get for you while I'm in Paris?"

Mary looked back and said, "You'll have quite enough to occupy you without worrying about me. Just make sure you enjoy yourselves."

***

Later that evening Mary spoke to Tom. "She will be twenty-one this month. But for all her education and common sense, she has no experience with boys or men at all. Please be careful with her."

"Mary, I became her boyfriend as a joke. At least that's what I thought at the time. I no longer consider it a joke. I believe that it was instinct that caused me to ask the question, and the same instinct made me happy with the answer. If things work out you may need to prepare for an addition to the family, providing your husband is agreeable."

Mary laughed, "You do not seriously believe that my husband would turn down a Grand Banks ticketed Mate as a grandson-in-law do you?"

Tom looked a bit flustered at her obvious amusement. "I... I thought he would be worried. It all happened so fast that I was worried! Surely Lotte must be worried too, whatever she says."

"Well, well. You obviously do not realise that Lotte decided that you would be the one for her more or less as soon as she saw you. That means that if you are the man she thinks you are, all will be well between you. If not, well, we all make mistakes. Just treat her gently, and ah," her voice wavered and Tom thought for a moment that she might cry. "Look after her."

Tom actually blushed.

The conversation ended at that point as Lotte came into the cabin wearing a white blouse and a blue skirt. Her hair was loose and fell down to her shoulders. Without make-up she stood in the middle of the cabin. "Well, will this do?" she said and spun round, causing the skirt to lift and show off her legs. Mary smiled and looked at Tom. He looked at Lotte and said, "Gorgeous!"

Lotte squealed and dropped onto his lap and hugged him. "Wow! Nobody has ever called me gorgeous before. Do you really mean it?"

"I certainly do. Mary, what do you think?"

"I think you're gorgeous, too." Mary said. "By the way, Tom, that is the first time I've seen Lotte's legs in seven years You are honoured."

"Oh, gran, please. That was not necessary. You'll embarrass the man."

"Let's get things sorted out now. I will get a car laid on for first thing in the morning, so that we get the maximum of time in Paris."

***

For Tom the next two days were best of times. He could not recall when he enjoyed himself more.

For Lotte it was a unique experience. Suddenly she was being treated as a woman by a good-looking, thoughtful man who was rapidly becoming her friend. Here she realised that though she had made friends with others in the past, there had not been the same electricity between them.

They had stayed in a small hotel in the Rue Parmentier. The twin-bedded room had been basic, but it was just right in the circumstances.

For Lotte the situation was both exciting and worrying at the same time. It was an anti-climax in one way when Tom made no effort to seduce her. She did not know whether to be happy or not in the circumstances. She was reassured when he held her close and kissed her goodnight before taking to his bed.

For Lotte, the ongoing noises of Paris coming through the window, combined with the strange bed, made sleeping difficult after the excitement of the day. Finally, she looked across at Tom. To her surprise she saw that he was looking at her. "Would you mind if I joined you?"

He said nothing but he threw the covers back. She went over and joined him. They slept cuddled together. She, happy to be safe in his arms in this strange place, he amazed at the way this girl/woman had so swiftly become so important to him.

***

Back at Le Treport they dropped off the purchases at the harbour office, while they returned the car to the hire company. Hand in hand they walked back, picked up their packages and walked down to the ship. Calling out to Mary, they bundled through to the saloon, dumping the packages on the table.

Tom suddenly realised that there was something wrong. Then he saw Mary's shoe under the table. As he dropped down to pick it up, he saw Mary's crumpled figure hidden from their view by the table.

He crawled under the table. To his relief he felt the pulse in her neck. "Lotte. I need help here!"

Lotte came through from her cabin. "What's up?" She looked around. "Where are you?"

"Under here!" Tom said. "Under the table. Its Mary. She's been hurt."

Lotte's startled face appeared. "What's wrong? Oh, Mary? What's happened?"

Tom said, "I need you to go to the office and call an ambulance. Oh, and call the police as well. Somebody has hit her with something. There is blood on the back of her head."

Lotte didn't wait. She dashed off to call for help, leaving Tom to look after Mary.

While they lay there, Mary came round.

"Just lie still, Mary. Relax and tell me if you hurt anywhere else, apart from your head?"

Mary said, "Ouch!" Touching her head gingerly. "They were looking for Will. They did not sound French." She stopped, wincing as she struggled to sit up.

Tom helped her, propping her against his shoulder. "Just take it easy, Mary. The medics will be here soon."

Lotte returned with the harbour master, who carried a first aid box. Between the two men they lifted Mary up onto the bench seat. The siren of an ambulance blipped and the Harbour Master left, to bring the Paramedics to the *Speedwell*.

Will arrived with the team. Lotte filled him in with what she knew.

Tom was not needed and appeared on deck. He told Will what Mary had said about the men looking for Will.

Will turned to Tom. "Prepare for sea. If Mary is up to it, we will leave as soon as the medics are finished. We cannot afford to get trapped here dealing with the police. We would be too vulnerable. I'll fix the harbour master. You two get cleared away to move as soon as they are all ashore.

Tom and Lotte went down the fore hatch and got changed into their sailing gear. Both were back on deck within a few minutes.

They were in time to see the harbour master and the two paramedics being bundled ashore by Will.

They had the craft cast off and moving out within minutes, barely scraping through the lock gates before the tide required them to close. Tom took the helm. Under power they headed out into the open sea, on a rough course west, en-route to La Rochelle.

Clear of the port, the navigation lights now lit, Lotte was loosening the ties on the flying jib. She released the roller reefing and hauled the sail out, setting it neatly, before running to the foresail to do similar service. As both sails started to draw, Tom switched off the engine, threw the loops over the wheel spokes and went to help with the main and mizzen sails.

Then he handed over to Lotte and went below to set a proper course. Using the Satnav, he plotted the mean course bearings and dashed back on deck. He called the amended course out to Lotte while he trimmed the sails. Once all were drawing to his satisfaction, he rejoined Lotte at the wheel. She looked at him fondly. "Food and coffee. I'll see what's happening below." She kissed him briefly and dashed off, leaving him alone with the stars, the lights from the shore, and the occasional ships in the dark waters of the Channel.

***

Lotte joined him with soup and sandwiches. putting the tray on the cabin roof beside them. "Granma is fine. She'll have a sore head for a while, but she is okay. Grandpa is with her, and we have the ship.

She gave him his soup and sipped her own. "Was I really gorgeous?" She whispered.

"You really were, and for me you always will be," Tom said. Lotte slipped her arms round his neck and kissed him slow and seriously.

***

In the light of morning it was possible to see the ferry from Southampton to Le Havre crossing their course ahead. Tom shook Lotte awake. "Take over for a while I'll get breakfast."

Lotte opened her eyes and stretched. "Must you go?"

But he was gone already. It was not long before the scent of frying bacon was mingling with the smell of the sea.

Will appeared at breakfast. Mary got up and found a place to relax and take advantage of the sunny weather they were enjoying, on the long stretch south-west from the Cherbourg peninsular.

It was she who noticed their shadow.

"Tom! Correct me if I am wrong. But is that another boat I see out there?" She pointed out to the west. There it was possible to see the slap of a hull into the waves sweeping in from the Atlantic.

Tom leaned into the radar, currently set on 5 mile range, and switched to 15 miles. The height of the main mast gave their radar a greater range than the average yacht. The white trace of the other boat was evident, paralleling their course about six miles out. He lifted his head. "You could be right. I'll take the glass and have a look from the mast head."

He collected the telescope from below, and hooked his harness to a rope that looped to a winch allowing maintenance to be carried out to the main mast.

He grinned at Mary and called out, "Reel me up, Lotte."

He rose up the mast as the winch took strain, and easily pulled him up to the joint for the mast stays. There he braced himself and opened the telescope to its full extent. Lining up with the distant white smear, he allowed himself to adjust to the movement of the ship before bringing the distant boat into focus. He saw the big power boat at the top of a wave. The familiar outline identified immediately. Then he closed the telescope and called to be lowered.

Once back on deck he called to Will and walked to where Mary sat. "It's the *Stroller,*" he said. "Peter Speight's boat, but what is it doing here?"

Will said, "He must have come through the Caledonian Canal to Fort William, then down the Irish Sea to have got here in this time."

Mary said, "Now tell me why he would do that?" She looked at her husband directly, "And while we are at it, why was I mugged by men looking for you?"

Will wriggled uncomfortably.

Mary said, "I won't ask again, Will. We need to know what we are into."

Will looked around at the others. He shrugged. "I'm sorry. I did not anticipate this. I was asked to do a delivery by a former colleague who is still with Naval Intelligence. It was just supposed to be a drop, better accomplished by a civilian.

"There was a complication. The contact was ambushed and only got away by the skin of his teeth. It meant that I was identified, apparently. I presume that was why they came on board looking for me when Mary was hurt."

Tom said, "What are we up against?"

Will looked embarrassed. "This needn't concern you. I have the problem. If you and Lotte go ashore there is no reason why you would need to become involved."

Tom looked directly at Will. "I signed on for the voyage. As far as I am concerned, that means 'come what may'. So where do we go from here?"

Lotte took his arm and squeezed it. "That goes for us both," she said.

Mary spoke up, "When you have all finished beating the drum, what do you suggest we do about our friends over there?" She nodded at the present location of the power boat shadowing them.

"There is nothing we can do during daylight that is for sure. What I can do is check with HQ and see what they suggest."

Mary said quietly, "The people who came to me had guns. How are we fixed?"

Will looked at her sharply. "Guns, we don't need guns!"

Mary looked at him patiently. "Will, if I had had a gun handy, I would not have been mugged!"

Will thought for a moment. He turned to Tom. "Have you ever used a hand gun?"

Tom smiled. "I was on the Grand Banks. I had a hand gun, and I used a rifle. We always travelled armed. There were pirates on the Banks, and I sailed in the Pacific to the Pribilof Islands. The Russians were not backward in coming forward if they saw a chance for a little extra profit. I suspect some of the Americans were not too choosey either."

"Perhaps you should come and look over our armoury." He led the way below and into saloon. He removed the board facing the built-in bench seat, and pulled out a drawer perhaps a foot deep. There had been no sign that there was a drawer there. The catch was under the mattress at the foot of the bunk.

In the drawer there were several weapons, four automatic pistols, and a Frontier Colt. There were four rifles, including a Winchester familiar from a thousand Western movies, a Lee Enfield mark 4 with sniper scope, an Armalite and a NATO model semi-automatic rifle, and finally two Uzi smg's.

"Wow! What is this for? World war three?" Tom was impressed.

"Anything catch your eye?" Will asked.

Tom selected the Glock from the handguns and the Armalite with the twelve-shot magazine from the long guns. He checked the Glock, and made sure it was loaded and ready before slipping it into the waistband of his trousers in the middle of his back.

Lotte called from her position on the cabin roof. "*Stroller* is closing the gap. There are several people on her deck."

Will got on the radio. "Stroller, Stroller, come in, please."

"Hullo, Speedwell. This is Stroller. Why don't you heave-to for a chat? Over." The voice of Peter Speight came over loud and clear.

"Stroller, Stroller, what are your intentions? Over"

"Just heave-to like a sensible man. You do have women aboard after all."

Chapter Three

Action and reaction

Tom heard the conversation and collected the Armalite. To his surprise Mary took the Lee Enfield, and Lotte the Uzi smg. Both handled the guns like old friends. Both lowered themselves to the deck at either end of the deckhouse, taking cover from the corners.

Meanwhile, Will Pleasance spoke once more. "Stroller, Stroller, you are warned to keep your distance. I will not be heaving-to. Nor will I respond to coercion."

The power boat was now 200 yards off the beam of the schooner. One of the men on deck fired a burst from his smg across the bow of *Speedwell.*

The crack of the Armalite raised a spray of splinters from the deck beside the feet of the machine gunner. He jerked in surprise at the sting of the splinters in his leg and dropped he weapon. It hit the coaming and hesitated, the boat rolled, and with a splash the weapon sank into the grey waters of the Channel.

"How dare you open fire on a British ship in open waters," Will called. "Mayday, Mayday, this is the schooner, *Speedwell*. I am under fire from pirates attempting to board my ship by force. I am 3 miles off Cap-de-la Hague."

"You are a fool, Pleasance. We could have solved all this here in private. Now we will have to put this off to another time and it may not be such a friendly occasion."

"Push off, Speight. Whoever you are working for has got to be anti-British. That means you are a traitor to your country. So get off before I riddle your engine room and leave you to sink in that jumped-up gin palace. Out"

Will poked his head out of the cabin, raising his middle finger erect at the big power boar off the starboard beam. The bullet flicked his hair as he stood there.

From the fore end of the deckhouse the Lee Enfield spoke. The helmsman on the power boat flinched and looked in astonishment at his hand. The bullet had passed through the wheel and the palm of his hand.

On the *Speedwell* Will sat on the steps out of sight of the shooter on the power boat. His face was white with shock. The bullet had passed an inch from his temple. The mizzen mast had a small hole where it had lodged.

The *Stroller* turned sharply away to starboard back toward the British shore, the stern digging deeper as the power was increased.

Mary appeared, trailing the rifle she had used. "First blood to us, I believe," she said calmly. "What's up with you? You look as if you've seen a ghost?"

Will pointed at the bullet hole in the mast and collected the little bunch of grey hairs from the deck.

"Oh, my god," Mary said. I did not realise." She hugged Will. "If I had known, I would have shot the engine out."

"Just as well you didn't know, then," Will said sharply. "How many do you think there were, Tom?"

"I counted five."

Lotte broke in. "I saw more below. I reckon eight. I didn't see Nadine though."

***

La Rochelle

Donny eased the wheel and steered the *Swallow* through the towers standing at the entrance to La Rochelle harbour. Abby reefed the fore sail and jib, then gathered the mizzen sail by hand, as the main-sail rolled down to a level which allowed the stiffeners to be removed before the sail could be harbour-stowed.

They were directed to moor against one of the pontoons in the marina. There were many gaps where boats were away for the season.

Abby leapt ashore and started tying-up, while Donny switched off the engine and eased his shoulders.

Once below he set-to tidying the cabin. Abby joined him, having hooked up to the service pillar on the pontoon deck. They did not waste too much time before departing for town and something to eat—which they did not have to prepare themselves.

"What did Jonathon have to say?" Abby said curiously.

The phone call had come as they were entering the harbour. Donny had groaned when he saw the sender was Jonathon Glynn, M16. Jonathon, a friend of Donny's father, had been involved in most of the escapades which Donny and Abby had been involved in. Donny grinned. "'You should not leave the country before informing us. You should let us know first, not when you are sailing into a foreign port'. I pointed out that, technically, La Rochelle is not a foreign port, but he was not listening. Basically he was just miffed to hear from home that we had sailed off into the sunset without telling him. We are expected to keep an ear to the ground while here. Something is stirring."

"I can tell from the pricking of my thumbs something wicked this way comes." Abby giggled, paraphrasing Shakespeare. "Poor Jonathon. Did you remind him that we were still on leave of absence?"

Donny shrugged, "What good would it have done?"

***

The *Speedwell* was already moored in La Rochelle. Will had gone ashore immediately to contact his people about the attack by the *Stroller*. With the ship locked up the others landed with a promise to meet at six pm to arrange dinner.

Tom kept the Glock tucked in his waistband, just in case. Mary went shopping on her own, leaving Lotte with Tom. They wanted to stroll around the old town, and perhaps have a look at the old U Boat base in the sunny weather.

***

Donny and Abby were eating alfresco, the evening was warm still, and lit up by the lights of the shops and restaurants as well as the street lamps. Both were engrossed in the passing parade of people and traffic, commenting from time to time on the activity around them.

The accident happened on the street in front of their table. Only it was not an accident. The victim was on the pavement walking down the street. The car started up and drove at her. Just like that.

Donny was on his feet immediately, calling out a warning to the woman who managed to avoid being hit more than a glancing blow.

Abby called for an ambulance, Donny raced down to try and stop, or at least identify, the car.

***

Abby saw Mary into the hospital, then made her way back to the marina. Will had already left for the hospital when Abby arrived at the *Speedwell's* mooring. She introduced herself to Tom and Lotte. "I'm Abby Marshall, from the ketch over there." She pointed across to the *Swallow*. I am here with my friend, Donny Weston. "We saw the attack on Mrs. Pleasance and got her to the hospital. Donny tried to stop the car but only managed to get the number. The lady has a broken arm, now plastered. Apart from cuts and bruises, she is otherwise unhurt. It was deliberate."

She told the full story to the two young people sitting in the saloon of the schooner. "We saw them earlier. They were parked. When Mrs. Pleasance came down the road they started up the engine. Though she was well clear of their path, they deliberately drove at her. Donny shouted to warn her and she nearly managed to avoid them completely.

"The car drove off straight away. Mrs Pleasance was surrounded by people at that point. Donny gave the number to the police. But I would bet the vehicle was either stolen or the plates are false."

***

Abby, Lotte and Tom sat waiting until Donny, Will and Mary returned. Donny and Will were briefly alone, while Mary was taken by the girls to change her battered clothes. Tom went to the galley to make coffee and sandwiches.

Donny said, "Will Pleasance, Intelligence?"

Will looked up sharply, "Commander RN, retired."

Donny said, "Remember Jonathon Glynn?"

Will commented, "I have been wondering why the names Donny and Abby sounded familiar. Jonathon, eh? That was the key. How is he these days? Working for that female martinet who took over the department, is he?"

Donny grinned, "Last time we spoke he was. As were we at the time. We are on leave of absence having finished our degrees. We are currently taking our ketch to the Med before we get dragged back into things."

The female contingent returned and Tom appeared with the sandwiches.

Will contributed little to the conversation until after they had eaten. Then the explanation was demanded by Mary. "Out with it, Will. We have these young people here being shot at without a hint of why! They put up with you. Obviously you know

Donny and Abby. I'm afraid it won't do for me. What is going on?"

Looking a little older than he had earlier, Will sat back against the cushions on the bench seat round the table. He drew out a Dutch cigar and lit it, considering what he could say, and how little he could get away with saying.

Eventually, when his cigar was lit and drawing to his satisfaction he said, "Here it is! Basically, my people, as you call them, do not have a clue as to the identity of these people attacking us." He lifted his hands at the storm of complaint rising at this remark. "Let me finish," he said impatiently. When they calmed down he began again. "Because my people knew nothing, I contacted an old friend in M16. I mentioned my mission for the Department. He was appalled. In his opinion they should never have used me for the transmission of data which was so sensitive. He will be in touch with some answers. But meanwhile, he is aware of the rise of a new organisation. They are international, using people from all over the world. He thinks it is deliberate. The individual governments must all be prepared to share data to have a chance to stop them. Like him, I don't hold out much hope for the chances of the governments cooperating successfully."

"Sounds serious. But what is it all about? That seems to be the bit you keep missing out on." Mary was determined to have an answer. Donny and Abby sat quietly saying nothing.

The others nodded their agreement with Mary, so Will shrugged his shoulders and told them.

"Three years ago there was an accidental breakthrough in the development of non-toxic fuels. We are not talking some new source of fossil fuel. We are talking a complete different source here. Like the ignored suggestion of producing hydroelectricity from the individual house water supply, there is a danger here of the formula being suppressed, as happens so often when efficiency gives way to profits.

"What is this then? Converting water into energy for an internal combustion engine?"

"As I have already said, it's from a non-toxic source and that is all I am saying."

"So who is after us? Are we talking governments or commercial companies, or even individuals? In the circumstances I do think we have a right to know." Tom's question was asked calmly and pointedly.

Will reply was succinct. "I don't actually know. But what I can tell you is, whoever it is has made it clear there are no holds barred in this little skirmish. From now on all of us must be armed and ready to react in the face of any threat from strangers, or, more significantly, people we know. Do you all understand?"

He looked at the serious faces in front of him searching for disagreement or misunderstanding. Finding none, he said, "Okay all, I'm tired. If you don't mind, I'll be off to bed."

Mary said, "Me, too. Goodnight to you all." She turned to Abby and took her hand. "Thanks to you and Donny, they missed this time. So please be careful both of you." Mary followed Will from the cabin, leaving the four young people together.

Lotte and Tom sat together in the saloon with Donny and Abby. Tom looked at Lotte searchingly "Are you ready to go to bed too?"

"Is that an offer?" She said with a grin.

"Not as such," he replied. "I did have something else in mind."

Lotte shrugged a little regretfully, "Right. What did you have in mind?"

Tom turned to Donny, "I think we are being watched! I also think that the people watching us are the ones that hurt Mary. I do not like these people and I intend to find them and hurt them. Perhaps they will learn to leave us alone. If they don't, then I will seriously hurt them."

"Sounds reasonable," Donny said. "They had to be aware of your movements so that they could set things up tonight."

"You two are serious, aren't you?" Lotte looked at Tom and Donny with interest. "I presume we will be armed, just in case they are armed?"

Tom nodded. "Are you interested?"

"No pulled punches?"

"Absolutely not!" Tom said emphatically.

"All right. You're on." Lotte sounded certain.

Donny said, "I'll need to get back to our boat, our weapons are there."

"Don't worry, we can manage."

Tom opened the arsenal and withdrew three more Glock automatics, a magazine and a spare for each. He checked them, slotted in the magazines loading the chamber, set the safety catch and handed the guns out one by one. He found four suppressors and added them to the issue. "There we are. Remember the safety catch. Now we drift around keeping our eyes open. Make no sign if you spot someone. There may be more than one so it will be a question of patience. But before we leave the ship, we will keep low and take a long look from cover on deck. Look for people who do not move about. Look for anyone who seems to be looking at us. If you spot any one, look for a partner. Then sneak back across the deck to the cabin. We will compare notes before we go hunting.

Donny and Abby went up on deck quietly. Lotte looked at Tom, then reached up pulled his head down and kissed him firmly on the lips. "Let's do it," she said.

They joined the others on deck keeping below the level of the bulwarks. Lotte stationed herself at the break where the bulwarks were broken by a section of railing. Tom settled for the break where the boarding ladder was set. Donny had gone forward and Abby aft.

The scattered lights from the many occupied boats in the marina made shadows fall in odd directions. It took time to settle and identify the real from the imagined. The watchers studied the visible area in front of them minutely, inching their glasses over the area, seeking the slightest movement which should not be there. Lotte spotted her watcher when a hatch was thrown open by one of the crew of a sixty-foot Sunseeker yacht. The light from the hatch caught the flutter of movement where none had been a moment before.

The hatch closed. But now she knew where to look, Lotte was able to make out the dark figure sitting crouched beside a mooring bollard on the far pontoon.

Lotte confirmed that the watcher was not shifting his place. After a few minutes she withdrew from her vantage point and slithered along the deck to Tom's place by the entry port.

Tom sat back and rubbed his eyes, "Over beside the gate, three boats down, crouched on the deck of the Westerly ketch with the British colours. "He muttered.

"Mine is over behind the big Sunseeker." Lotte contributed.

"Call in the others."

In the cabin Donny confirmed both sightings.

Lotte asked, "How do we go about this?"

Donny said, "We drop off together. Use the suppressors on the weapons, so that if we have to shoot we won't wake up the area. Keep in touch with the headsets. Tap twice when you are in position and wait for my signal before you act." He looked at Lotte. "You sure you're up to this?"

"I'm sure." The voice was steady, no tremor. She looked him in the eye. Abby smiled and nodded to Donny.

Tom looked back for a moment, and then he leaned down and kissed Lotte. As he straightened the thought occurred that he could get used to kissing this girl/woman, who had unexpectedly entered his life in such an odd way.

***

Led by Donny, Tom, Lotte and Abby slipped overboard into the long shadow along the pontoon beside the schooner. At the T junction they separated, turning in different directions, Tom and Lotte heading completely around the marina to reach the location of their watcher. Donny and Abby had a more direct, but also more observable, route to reach their objective.

***

Patrick Berger watched the TV idly as he sat at his desk in the company office. His partner, Alice Mills, was reclining gracefully on the settee on the other side of the office, her legs drawn up partially underneath her. In positioning them, she had inadvertently exposed a little more leg than she intended, a fact brought home to her by her discreet observation of the looks her partner kept taking in her direction. She was aware of the effect she had on him. She often played to it to get her own way. On this occasion she left things as they were, even enjoying the fact that she was distracting him to the extent that he was not keeping as close an eye on the ongoing task as he should have.

Tiring of the game, she sat up with a flirt of white lace as she straightened her legs. "What is happening?" She said, "Have they made a move yet?"

His eyes had picked up the movement of her legs. He consequently missed the faint flicker of movement when Tom was forced to pass through a dimly lit area on his way to the watcher near the marina gate.

"Nothing doing at the moment!" Berger said. "They are probably in bed enjoying each other, while we sit wasting our time when we could be doing the same thing."

"Still dreaming, I see," Alice said drily.

The radio on the desk by the TV squawked and went silent.

"What was that?" Alice said.

Berger looked at the screen intently. "Come in, Ob1?"

There was no answer. "Ob2, report please?" Once more there was no answer.

"Shit!" Berger said. "They've been spotted and neutralised." He switched off the sets and made for the door with Alice right behind him.

They were too late of course. They found Ob2 trussed up on the pontoon. Of Ob1 there was no sign. It was not surprising. Ob1 was, at the time, seated in the rear of a container which had once been used for storage of cleaning materials used on the boats in the next door boatyard. He was wondering where he was. He was not reassured by the two masked people facing him.

"Who employed you?" The voice was deep and menacing.

Henry O'Connor was a hired hand. From the sound of it his inquisitor was a hard man. "C.I.A.," he said quickly.

"What were you told to do? Report on this?"

He nodded his head rapidly. "She said I was to tell her if anyone got off the schooner in the marina."

"How long had you been there?"

"We arrived tonight, about seven pm."

"Do you always carry this?" The other person lifted up the Walther PPK he had been armed with."

"Usually. This is a dicey business I'm in."

"What about your partner? Did he have one too?"

"I think so." The voice was getting a little frazzled.

"How did you know they were CIA?"

"That bit was easy. Everyone knows who they are in this area. They are always doing this sort of thing, checking up on illegals and running hi-jack operations against the local gangs."

"Hi-jacking, did you say?"

"Hi-jacking drugs. Sometimes people. They are well known and not trusted among the local villains."

"Why do you work for them?"

"We need the money. It always seems to lead to the money, one way or another. I am beginning to despair for the human race."

Lotte said, "What do we do with him? Shoot him?

Their captive looked alarmed.

Tom looked at him long and searchingly. Slowly he shook his head. "It's an idea. I do not like being watched."

The man was now getting really uncomfortable. Tom was rubbing his chin still thinking out loud. "What else can we do with you?" He asked.

"How would it be if I go on holiday to Marseilles for a month or so? I have family there I haven't seen for a while. They would be pleased to see me."

"Sounds like a plan. However your employers may not be happy?"

"Fuck them! It was us sitting in the Marina."

"Marseilles sounds reasonable to me." Tom said. "What do you think, Lotte?"

"Let him go. If I see him again, I'll shoot him."

"Before you go, where do I find these CIA people?" Tom asked.

"Two streets back, number 17," the man said without hesitation.

They watched him trot off through the boatyard exit from the marina. As he left they saw two people rising to their feet having released the other watcher.

Without revealing their presence they watched the pair leave through the front gate, following the other discomforted watcher.

Lotte and Tom followed the pair people at a distance. Knowing where they were going meant that they did not have to stay close. Donny and Abby joined them as they reached the CIA house. They waited until the door closed. Then Donny produced picks and slipped the lock on the front door. He opened the door quietly and slipped through, closely followed by the others. There was no sound from the downstairs section of the house though there was the sound of activity upstairs.

They crept up the stairs, Donny leading, gun in hand. At the top of the stairs the noises were coming from the room at the front of the house. Tom checked the room at the rear and the bathroom. Both were empty. At the door to the front room Donny looked at the others. Donny nodded and reached for the door handle.

Chapter four...Making Waves

As the door crashed open the two people inside reached for their weapons. "Don't!" Donny said. Both froze and the hands dropped to their sides. "Now just lift the weapons out with two fingers and drop them on the bed." His voice was quiet but firm. Both Berger and Alice complied without attempting any other moves. Tom collected the guns and Abby frisked Alice. Tom searched Berger.

"Right. Now tell us why you are so interested in us?"

Neither Berger nor Alice volunteered any answer.

"I really think it's will be necessary for you to let us know why you are surveilling us. Also perhaps you can explain why an attempt was made to knock over Mary Pleasance. It was pure luck that the attempt did not succeed. As it was, her arm was broken. Have you any comment to make?"

"Only that it was nothing to do with us," Berger volunteered.

"Where did that happen?" Alice asked.

"Here in La Rochelle. The van did not stop." Tom's voice was hard.

"That was not our people. We have no reason to do things like that. Someone else is involved in this operation. My guess would be the Russians.

"We are still awaiting your reply." Tom said.

"About what?" Alice asked.

"Stop pissing about. What is this all about? Why were you watching us?" Lotte was sounding very impatient.

They searched the place, there seemed to be nothing there of interest.

"Let's get them back to the boat, we can chat more easily there."

In two groups of three, the six people walked down to the marina and boarded Donny and Abby's boat. *Swallow*.

The water lapped alongside the hull, the four people were sitting looking at each other across the cabin. Both CIA agents were still tied up, their hands in front of them, sitting on the cabin floor.

Tom turned to Donny. I'm fed-up with this, let's just tip them into the harbour. They don't want to tell us why they are watching us. There is nothing else we need them for and I don't trust them. They were watching us and they haven't convinced me that they had nothing to do with the attack on Mary."

Donny looked thoughtfully at the other pair. "I think I agree with you."

The captives were looking apprehensively at each other.

Tom started to rise to his feet.

Alice broke! "Tell them, Berger. If you don't I will."

"Now, Alice..." Berger began.

"We suspected that the Commander was holding out on us, possibly selling us out to the Russians or possibly to the Chinese. We had orders to keep a look out for and stall any attempt by the Commander to contact anyone about the information he has."

"And what might that be?" Donny asked casually.

Alice hesitated, "It, it's classified."

"Okay, Tom. Let's toss them overboard." Donny sounded really angry.

Desperately, Alice said. "It's about the latest jet engine. They have found a way of running it by some explosive spark system, apparently."

"That's it. Both into the harbour. Now." Tom stood fully and reached to pull Patrick Berger from the floor as he was pulling back, trying to keep out of reach.

"Tell them, for Pete's sake," he said desperately. "I do not need a swim without the use of my arms and legs."

Alice said, "But…"

"Tell them! Now!" He had been hauled to his feet by the two men.

Alice shouted, "It's some bloody power source using non-toxic elements that are freely available."

Tom thrust Berger back in his seat. "Who are you really working for?"

"UNOCON!" Both captives replied in unison.

***

"Uzbekistan Natural Oil Consortium," Will said reflectively, "No. That is the second fall-back. The real answer will be probably a government, though not Uzbekistan or even USA. My feeling is probably the Middle-East."

Having roused Will out next morning, Tom exhibited the two captives to his skipper. Will had taken one look at the disgruntled pair and returned to the saloon.

After some thought he said, "They probably are CIA. Their agents all seem to suffer from the illusion that whatever part they play makes them immediately part of the passing scene. The problem is terminal delusion in many cases. Like this pair, the part they play is 'spook'. Thus they tell the world that they are CIA because all the other agencies do a better job of blending in."

"Do I let them go?" Tom asked doubtfully.

"Yes, quietly. That way they will probably keep this all to themselves. That way they won't get replaced, so we will always know who they are. It could save us having to identify their replacements. Also we may be able to use them."

Tom nodded thoughtfully and went below to release their captives.

"We have not reported this incident. It's up to you what you do or say about it." He looked at Berger's swollen eye, "How did that happen?"

Alice smiled. "He didn't listen to me. That is not the only swollen part of his anatomy."

Tom cut the plastic handcuffs. As they stood he noticed Berger wince. Apparently Alice had not shared their incarceration the way Patrick expected her to.

He escorted them ashore, refusing their requests for papers and weapons. "I am sure you will manage somehow. I don't see why I should go out of my way to help you."

He watched the two bedraggled figures make their way out of the marina before returning to the saloon.

***

Donny and Abby came over as the CIA pair departed. Donny turned to Abby, "Well, what do we do? Do we do the usual, or be sensible over this one?"

Abby looked at Donny shrewdly. "You do not fool me, lover. You have every intention of poking your nose into this can of worms. I can see Tom and

Lotte are good, but neither of them is professional. Will you ring Jonathon or shall I?"

The call took a little longer than they expected. Jonathon was not in the office. Nor was he at home. When Donny put the phone down shrugging his shoulders, it rang.

Abby picked up. "Hello, Jonathon!" she said quietly. "We are moored in the marina straight out along the main pontoon, Take the first right. We are the fourth boat, and, yes, it is still the *Swallow*. Ten minutes."

She put the phone down and turned to Donny. "Put the kettle on. He'll be here in ten minutes."

Jonathon seemed harassed. His hair was mussed a little, which was most unusual for him. It seemed that there had been an altercation at the station when he had arrived in France, something to do with identity documents. Jonathon had been struck by a flying fist. Annoyed by the officer involved, Jonathon had flattened him with one punch and spent the next ten minutes explaining to the police that he had been assaulted, and his retaliation was justified. This caused him to miss his train. As a result he had been required to drive the entire distance.

He explained all this to Abby as he was carefully brushing the errant strands of hair back into their proper place.

"Why did you not just get the next train? You would have arrived several hours ago." Donny asked innocently.

Jonathon looked at Donny suspiciously. "I decided it would be more practical to have a car available," he said acidly. "Now can I have an update on what is happening here?"

Abby smiled and said, "Why, Jonathon, I thought that you were here to brief us."

"You rang me, remember?" He said sharply.

"Ten minutes ago!" Abby said. "We are here on holiday. I presume that not being Superman, you were almost here when I rang. I repeat. What are *you* doing here?"

Jonathon shrugged. "Since you are already here, I suppose I can use you for some small tasks."

"Please do not put yourself out. We have some friends here who are in trouble. We will just help them out and forget you were ever here." Donny's sarcastic comments accompanied his nod to Abby, who immediately started to move out of the cabin.

"All right, I give in. I was coming here to warn you to stay out of the CIA's business. Since you are already in it up to your necks, there is not much point in doing that. So I'll lay the situation out for you and you can fill-in details as you know them.

"What we have here is a situation that has come out of inter-service rivalry. The CIA discovered a conspiracy to steal the formula for non-toxic fuel to replace current fuels to be used with variant internal combustion engines. It seems that the CIA, FBI and Homeland agents had all became aware of this threat and independently took action. The result was a complete balls-up. All three agencies crossed lines and none of them would step back to give the others a clear field." He stopped to see if they were still with him.

Abby said, "So how did the UNOCON people get involved in this little dispute?"

Jonathon looked up at the mention of UNO-CON. "So you know they are involved. I was just coming to them. Someone on one of the agencies gave the game away. Whoever did stands to win big time financially. However his life insurance had better be paid up, because when he is found his family will need something to keep them afloat."

"Where is the formula now? Why is it still floating about?" Donny sounded mystified and felt it.

Jonathon shrugged his shoulders. "It's pretty safe at the moment. Split into three sections. All three are needed to get the thing organised, I understand."

"Tell me why, in 2014, we still deal with idiots who have such outdated ideas as this one. Three sections? That is three chances to lose the whole thing entirely. Three chances to get together all three sections from people, rather than having to break into a well-guarded vault. Or better still who not manufacture the stuff and stop this nonsense altogether. Don't answer! Money, that's what it's all about. Greed. And, because of it, men and women have to risk their lives to protect a secret that could be worth a fortune, but is unlikely to benefit us, the ordinary people of the world, in any case."

Jonathon held his hands up. "What can I say? There is no answer to that. It's the way of the world as we know it."

"Where are we now as far as security is concerned? Who has what?"

"So far," said Jonathon. "We still have all the parts. The problem is one of the parts is somewhere between here and the lab. There, the delivery will allow the early production of sufficient material to convince the world that the stuff works.

"Problem! The opposition know where the stuff is going, so ambush is on the cards unless we can do something about it."

"What happened to the 'keep them out of things' bit, 'do not let them get involved' order. You have got to be sticking your neck way out." Abby sounded serious.

"You forget, my dear girl. I know where the bodies are buried."

"You should," retorted Donny. "You put most of them there!"

"So what are we supposed to be doing?" Abby persisted.

Jonathon sighed and ran his hands through his once more mussed hair. "First, make sure the Commander and Mrs. Pleasance are kept safe."

"You seem to have ignored our comments on what is actually happening. Lotte and Tom have been doing a pretty good job, since they realised that the danger existed." Donny made the point.

"True, but they are not trained agents." Jonathon said impatiently.

"And they have not been officially briefed, I suppose!" Abby snapped. "Get a life, Jonathon. These people have been coping in the dark, but they have been coping. With or without briefing, they have managed to counter two trained CIA agents, and they took part in driving off the power boat owned by Peter Speight. They are talented people. They will not be pushed around and they are not idiots. Like Donny and me, they deserve to know what we are really up against. This rubbish story about non-toxic fuel is about as real as my Aunt Fanny. So give it a rest and tell us the truth, or we will withdraw from the scene and get on with our voyage to Malta." Abby sat back, white-faced and angrier than Donny had ever seen her.

The shocked Jonathon looked as if he did not know what to do, which was probably the case. Donny almost felt sorry for him until he remembered the misinformation they had been given, and the real danger that threatened their new friends on the *Speedwell*. It occurred to him that the Commander Will Pleasance may have known the true facts. But it was possible he didn't.

"So, Jonathon, what is it going to be? Are we in or out?" Donny put the question.

Jonathon was looking harassed. "In, I suppose. This must be strictly between ourselves. The Commander has only been given the cover story."

"So the fuel business is all rubbish?" Abby said.

"Not entirely, but it has nothing to do with the real issue here. It was a convenient excuse, to set up our part of the operation."

"The CIA and the others involved, do they know?"

"I hope not. There has been a certain amount of double dealing going on between the CIA and the target."

Abby and Donny looked at each other. They turned on Jonathon together. "Target?"

Wearily, Jonathon sat back. "Drink, please. It's been a long day and I need sustenance."

"Jonathon! No food. No drink. Talk."

"His name is Oskar Renko. A so-called independent agent. A killer for hire. Espionage for a fee. Now, can I have something to eat and a drink, please?"

Donny poured out whisky for Jonathon, while Abby put the remains of the shepherd's pie they had had for lunch under the grill. They allowed Jonathon to eat before returning to the subject.

"Who is this Oskar Renko?" Abby asked.

"Think Carlos, the Jackal. There are maybe three men in the world, 'Bin Laden', Oskar Renko, and Carlos. Of course there are others, many others, but only these three were the sort of international figures who gave them work and notoriety. Oskar is, we are told, the only one left.

"There are a few complications. We discovered that the agency has retained Oskar to find a few things out for them. As a result he is operating under their protection, albeit temporary."

He sat back and collected his thoughts. "What has really complicated things is that one of the lines of enquiry Oskar has undertaken is across an investigation we ourselves are carrying out. We spoke to the cousins (CIA) on the subject and got the heave ho. We decided accordingly to give them a bloody nose. All would have been well if things had stopped there, but just like a bunch of kids, they threatened us. Only they actually carried out their threat and interfered with our negotiations with other European partners.

"That's when it really hit the fan. The pair of local agents are just obstructive, nothing else. Others have actually taken an aggressive attitude and are making efforts to interfere with activities involving our secret service. We are aware that this is initiated by a man called Remington, Paul Remington, who is an area supervising agent concentrating on France in particular but Europe in general.

"The reason we started this scam was that CIA i.e., Remington is operating outside the box. His boss knows nothing of this and we believe he is in cahoots with Oskar Renko. The only way we could get round the system without alarming Remington was to set up the trail of the non-toxic fuel. None of the information being allowed out in the open is actually relevant. It all applies to a system that failed in the past."

"That includes the information that Will Pleasance was carrying?" Donny mentioned.

"Yes, it did. We have made arrangements to prevent them getting further involved." Jonathon mentioned almost as an aside.

Abby said seriously, "We will have to do something about Tom and Lotte. I think we have to come clean about what is going on. They have been shot at and seriously interfered with, and remember, Mary suffered two events, including being run over and a broken arm." Abby said seriously.

Donny added, "In all fairness, Tom and Lotte are well capable of active service. They were doing all right before we came along. All things being equal I would suggest that they would be worth recruiting into the service."

"Can you work with them?"

"We already have. So the answer is 'yes'." Donny said. "Though I do agree Mary and Will should be placed somewhere safe for the near future. They are both vulnerable. Age and fitness are against them."

"I can and have officially excluded them. Meanwhile the best I can offer to you two at the moment is an address in Gueret and a blind eye to the assistance given by Tom and Lotte. I will look into the possibility of recruiting them, but you are aware of the handicap I have in the office."

It was known to both of them that the current head of Service not only disliked them, she also resented Jonathon's connections throughout the service, including the PM. He left the pair discussing their plans and went through to the forward berth where he crashed out, exhausted after a long day and night.

Chapter four...The Hunt

"Let's get together with Tom and Lotte." Abby pulled out her cell phone and called Lotte. When Lotte answered, she said, "Would you and Tom like to pop over for a drink? Our visitor has gone to bed, but Donny and I are wide awake. So how about it."

She heard the murmur of voices at the other end of the line, then, "We'll be right over. Start pouring."

***

Tom and Lotte sat comfortably on the saloon of the *Swallow* with drinks, a beer for Tom and G&T for Lotte. Donny and Abby were both drinking red wine.

Between them, Abby and Donny brought the other two up to date.

"Why tell us?" Lotte ventured.

The two agents exchanged looks. Then Donny spoke. "You two are already involved in this business, whether you like it or not. The type of people we are talking about are not inclined to take chances. In our experience, that means someone has you marked as players and therefore targets, certainly possible obstacles in their pursuit of the prize."

Abby added, "Your grandparents became involved when Will was employed as a messenger. They are going back to protected status in UK until this business is concluded. You can accompany them if you would rather, or you could join Donny and me in putting the entire matter to bed. Your choice." She sat back and sipped her wine looking at the pair opposite.

Tom said, "Surely the CIA are not really interested in us?"

Donny said, "Not only the CIA, I'm afraid. All the other interested parties will now be on the lookout for you. In effect, like us you will already be marked for attention, if not for removal. Staying in this vicinity will be dangerous, if you are not armed and ready to defend yourselves. One of the penalties of this game is that the people who play have no qualms about eliminating people they regard as threats to their own security. Remember the attacks on Mary, who could only have been of minimal interest to them? Think ruthless and you have a chance of survival. However on the up side, we..." He indicated Abby and himself, "have managed to keep ahead of the game for the past several years, and, incidentally, despite it being scary on occasion, we have managed to make a difference here and there."

"You are agents?" Tom said finding it difficult to accept, even taking into account what they had recently gone through.

Abby said "We were recruited when we were sixteen, mainly because, like you, we fell into a situation and reacted to it. It led to a series of events that we had no control over. We found ourselves targets, for no apparent reason, just like you two. Our reaction was to go on the offensive, and here we are nearly five years later, still alive and kicking with a series of..." she shrugged. "Shall I say, deactivated threats behind us."

There was a period of silence broken eventually by Lotte. "Do we get a badge?" The smile as she said it was reassuring. Tom grinned, "And a Walther PPK?"

"Perhaps. After we get issued with ours," Donny said with a grin. "We obviously haven't qualified yet."

Abby said, "I presume that means you are in? Remember, there are no guarantees in this business. Jonathon is our control but we only got temporary membership until last year when we were finally placed on the list. We are just beginning training to be barristers. I presume we will start in our trade, unless and until we are needed again. Meanwhile I suggest we get down to planning."

"The activities of Paul Remington are causing our people concern. He seems to be involved with serious industrial espionage. Somehow a deal between Oskar Renko and Remington is believed to be possibly lethal to a large section of the public." Donny lifted his hands. "Don't ask. I don't know nor does Jonathon. We are in the hunch area at present, so just hope like hell that our hunch is wrong."

"What would you like us to do?" Tom asked.

"Move to Gueret and survey the territory, but altered appearance, I think. You will have been photographed for sure, so we will adjust your appearance and send you both in. Abby, you travel with Lotte and Tom as backpackers."

"Good idea. How about you?"

"I'll think of something, perhaps a businessman. I'll check in to a hotel. Probably the Campanile. As a businessman I should not stand-out there.

"We have an address in town for Oskar and I'll see what we can do about Remington, a photo and/or some sort of address. Meanwhile do not go out unarmed, and do not go out alone at present. We will work out your change of appearance tomorrow, before we move off."

Abby sighed. "It might be an idea to have an early night before we take the plunge tomorrow." She looked at their two guests. "Getting to know each other faster than you anticipated, I suspect. Danger has that effect."

***

The world of Paul Remington was shrinking. His private life had gone to hell with the departure of his wife. He had been married for three years to Carlotta, another member of the agency, when they had their first child. His wife had been an all-round athlete and had the figure of Marilyn Monroe. Their child, Charles, was a golden child in most ways. Fair-haired and athletic, he was bright and talented. Carlotta recovered quickly from the birth and was once more the beauty she had always been.

The accident had been just that, an accident. The slate from the roof did not direct itself to their son, but it found him anyway. He died in the ambulance. The storm-loosened slate had been poised for some time according to the repairman. The day it slipped and killed Charles, a flirt of wind had been all it took.

Carlotta took it hard. She blamed Paul, herself, the weather and the job. She let herself go and the trim beauty became someone else. The marriage did not survive. Carlotta disappeared. When she returned she was once more the beauty, but no longer his. It became Paul's turn to drop out, but in his case he took a different direction. The asset, Oskar Renko, came under his direction. The agency, to save embarrassment, had transferred him to Europe while Carlotta worked from Washington.

The relationship with Renko was never close, but opportunities for profit began to present themselves. Paul found himself taking advantage where he could. It took three months for Paul to realise that Oskar Renko was running him, not the other way round. With the threat of disclosure over his head, Paul Remington found it easier to go along with Renko. His part in Renko's activities became more and more involved. Using his position in the CIA, he made funds and information available for Renko to use. His team of agents were used for purposes never intended by Washington. While Paul Remington had been known to feel shame, there was no way he would stop what he was doing. He was not impressed with the stories about the non-toxic fuel formula, recognising the pattern of a diversion from past experience. The UNOCON people had insisted on the research being done. The consequent capture and elimination of some of the people involved had merely exposed the ruthless nature of the producers of the diversion, and the greed and ruthlessness of the fuel producers. To be honest, Remington had not yet managed to winkle out the underlying reason for the diversion. Until he had clarified that, he was prepared to allow it to continue.

***

Oskar as always kept his cards close to his chest. Whether he realised the operation of the scam or not, nobody would know until he allowed them to know. He was almost an archetypal villain, swarthy, medium height, dark eyes and pockmarked face. His clothes generally looked as if he had slept in them. It was in fact often the case. He had a voracious appetite for women. The biggest surprise to those that knew him. Despite his appearance he seemed to attract them with little difficulty.

***

The house in Gueret was old and big, standing in its own grounds, detached and private behind walls and hedges, the occasional tree backing the protective barriers of stone and leylandii. The gates were antique but none the less forbidding, constructed from wrought iron coated with several generations of black paint, their hinges suspiciously smooth after all these years and responsive to the touch of a remote control with almost silky reaction. When closed, the additional discouragement of an electric charge was there to dissuade nosy intruders.

The house itself was furnished beautifully, but, sadly. the maintenance had been seriously neglected. Oskar Renko had a pathological distrust of hired help, depending on the inept services of his security team to keep the house going.

Remington always stayed at the Campanile when he was in town, preferring not to use the tacky facilities of the 'Manoir', so-called because the name board had lost half of its length and the 'de Quatre Vents' was no longer to be found. So the

Manor House of the four winds was now just the Manor House.

The staff comprised armed security men and women. Since they were on the move most of the time, intruders required heroic effort to pass through what was in fact a moving curtain of armed guards. The disadvantage, as far as the occupants were concerned, was the assumption that no one would be stupid enough to take on these odds.

An audacious intruder therefore had an opportunity to defeat security and, if inclined, shoot the target. Getting out would be something else.

***

The briefing session in the morning was attended by Jonathon. It was to him they had turned to establish the ground rules of the operation.

His answer to the question was, "There are no ground rules. We would like to capture the occupant Oskar Renko, If it is not possible, he should be killed."

The four people attending the briefing were not really ready for that remark. Donny made the comment. "Killed? Just like that, no trial? No defence?"

"No trial and no defence. The reason may seem obscure to you all. But if I mention that there is absolute proof, including a videoed admission of responsibility for the three bombings in Paris, London, and Washington, carried out during the last two years and the threatened attack on the Black

Sea site for the Olympic Games that was thwarted by accident when a dog pissed on the on the bomb and ruined the fuse. Oskar Renko has murdered more people than you know between you. The total numbers hundreds. He is currently working with the CIA on a project, His control is a man called Paul Remington. His bosses refuse to believe that the man has gone freelance. He is, technically, the agent in charge for the area of the European Union."

"What do we do about him if we come across him?" Tom said.

"I would not be unhappy if he had an accident. Depend on it; he would have no hesitation in removing you if you are in his way or, if he realises you intend taking Oskar Renko into custody."

"What it means is that we need to keep our wits about us and get in and out fast. Gun battles usually end up with people getting hurt. We need to have a good idea for getting into the Manoir and out again, without being rumbled. Failing that, without getting captured." Donny sounded serious and was in fact very serious. The Manoir would be no pushover.

"What about taking him outside the grounds? Does he ever leave the place? Has he a girlfriend? What do we know about him?" Abby interjected at this point.

"That would make sense. We need to get surveillance organised as fast as possible." Donny said,

"Have we a map of the area and the house in particular?"

Jonathon pushed a wad of maps onto the table. "I got these for the briefing. They include the architect's drawings of the house."

They spread the map out first and located the house and its closest neighbours,

"We have the latest Google map of the grounds and it does look as if things haven't changed much since they were produced."

Abby unrolled the drawings. Ignoring the elegant frontage, she pulled out the floor-plans to show the arrangement of the rooms within. The plans were recent. The modifications and upgrading had been carried out recently, apparently prior to the occupation by the present people.

Chapter five...Snatch

The black van stopped at the gates and the driver swore. "What the hell....."

The gateman walked to the driver's door of the van, tapped the window and motioned the driver to open it.

Cursing, the driver stabbed the button and the window slid open, allowing the cool evening air into the van.

The gateman thrust a clipboard toward the driver. A pen, attached by a piece of string, swung and clattered against the bodywork. "Sign for three men out 19.25." The voice was flat and emotionless."

The driver hauled in the pen and scrawled on the sheet. "We checked out by phone from the house!" he complained, "Where did all this rubbish come from?"

"Boss Oskar direct!" The gateman said. "If you've got a complaint make it to him."

He stepped back into his hut and the gate silently opened. While the van started up once more four figures in black from head to foot slipped through the opening gate below the eye level of the driver and out of sight of the gateman.

In the shelter of the shrubbery, Donny whispered, "That was lucky. Normally the gates open as the van approaches. There would have been less time for us to get through."

"It makes sense. Changing the routine keeps people on their toes!" Tom added.

"When you two finish demonstrating how smart you are, we are getting cold here waiting to move on!" Abby sounded impatient.

"Right move out. Keep in touch and pass on what you see." Donny's voice was serious through the personal talk system each of them wore. "Use the infra-red before you move."

Each had a pair of small binoculars, the left eye fitted with infra-red viewer to pick–up heat sources.

Tom squeezed Lotte's hand and split left. Lotte waited with Abby as Donny went right. two minutes later Abby gave Lotte a hug and made off right while Lotte went left. Donny spoke quietly, "Are you all in position?"

The other three acknowledged. Donny said, "Move out. Go now!" The four intruders started making their way toward the house, moving carefully from cover to cover.

In the house the man watching the detectors for the outside area, saw something and pressed the call button. The supervisor came, his jacket open and the gun visible in its underarm rig. He had a sand-wich half-eaten in his hand and when he reached the watcher he was still chewing. "What?" He said eyes on the screen but seeing nothing out of the ordinary.

"I saw something," the watcher said. "I was not sure what but there was something. Now it's gone."

"Probably an animal, we got foxes, you know." The supervisor stayed for a few minutes but nothing else appeared. He left, finishing his sandwich as he went.

Abby found the sensor in the bush beside her a fraction before she froze. The flicker of movement the watcher had seen was the impact of the spray when it hit and froze it for ten seconds, giving Abby time to move away.

The watcher continued his shift, He caught an-other flick of movement elsewhere in the grounds. He took a second, then a third look, but there was re-occurrence of the flick. This time he shrugged. He wouldn't bother his supervisor, it was probably some fox.

The guard stopped for a smoke in the shelter of the back porch. He was big and looked tough. *Asian possibly Korean,* Abby thought. She was almost under the man, lying below the edge next to the two steps up to the door level. She drew her suppressed Glock and snicked off the safety catch. The man walked to the steps and drew on his cigarette, look-ing out over the garden. He turned and looked down for the first step and saw her lying there, gun up. He began to open his mouth. The bullet went straight up entering his head beneath his chin and exiting through the top of his head. He collapsed like a tree, toppling down onto the path below the porch. The noise was lost in the night sounds.

Abby rolled him over, collected his gun and radio, then with great difficulty dragged him under the edge of the porch where he was half hidden at least. It was the best she could do.

Another watcher felt the cold touch of the gun to his neck. It shocked him. It was followed by a hiss, as the directed ether spray went straight into his nose and open mouth. He gasped and collapsed to the floor, unable to make his hands work, or control his legs.

Abby smiled under her face mask, It not only covered her face. It included a gas mask. She dragged the inert body over to the settee, bound his wrists and ankles, shifted the settee out and rolled him between it and the wall. She was pleased she had not needed to kill him as well.

Satisfied he was out of sight, she called the others. "I'm in the control room. The guard and the watcher are secure.

***

There were seven guards allocated to the house at the time, with the grounds outside under the surveillance of the electronic watcher. The guards spent very little of their time looking out of the windows or patrolling outside. When the van left it took two of the strength, a third was lying under the edge of the porch. One was behind the settee. The remaining three bodyguards were playing cards in the ready room, beside the study where Oskar spent most of his time. The supervisor was not of the group who were all CIA. He was private security, part of the team who normally protected the house and its occupants. The watcher and the gateman were part of his staff also, as was a backup watcher. He and the supervisor were in the security room. Jules Michel, the supervisor, looked at the man sleeping, and considered waking him and giving the duty man a break. He decided he would do it himself. The sleeping man was due on in 90 minutes. He would relieve Charles himself. He should practice a little, it had been some time since he had pulled a duty on the screens. He rose to his feet. From habit he pulled out his Star automatic and checked it was cocked and the safety was on. Replacing it, he straightened his jacket, doing the centre button up and walked through to the surveillance room. As he opened the door he saw the slender figure looking at the screen, no sign of the watcher on duty. The movement had warned the intruder, but the practiced supervisor had retrieved his automatic. It was pointing at the masked figure facing him.

"Who are you? What are you doing here?"

Abby stepped forward, ignoring the weapon. "I was just passing and I thought I would drop in on my friend. But he is not here. Have you seen him? She stepped forward once more, casually closing the distance between them. She noticed it was a Star automatic, Spanish made, a copy of? She could not remember which, but she did recall the safety catch. It was badly sited and easy to mis-set. She nodded at the gun in Michel's hand. "That's a Star, isn't it? The one with the faulty safety catch."

Jules Michel could not help glancing at the gun in his hand. He immediately realised that he should not. But too late. Abby's boot caught his extended wrist and the gun was gone, flying across the room to fall behind the monitors. The follow-up donkey kick caught him under his jaw. He thought, *I really should have continued my self-defence course.* Then there was no thought as he hit the wall behind him, already unconscious.

Abby recovered the Star automatic from behind the monitors. As she tied her latest victim up the others began to arrive.

Donny looked at the damaged man and grinned. "I've got three places where there are hot spots. One room down here has one, and there is an upstairs single. I'm guessing that may be friend Oskar. If I take Tom, will you and Lotte look after the others? The single is in the room two doors down.

The room with the three people is at the end of this corridor. "

Abby nodded. "Lotte, outside to the window where the single person is. I'll go in through the door. Abby waited until Donny and Tom went off, then walked down the hall to the door of the watchers' rest room. She opened the door gun in hand. There was a sleeping man on a cot in the corner. No-one else.

Abby smiled. Pulling her mask down again, she produced the ether spray, and pointing the nozzle at the sleeping man's face, she squeezed the button. The sleeping man inhaled the gas, coughed and half woke, but he was breathing in between coughs. He sank back on the bed, out for the count.

Abby called Lotte to go and report on the layout in the room where the other three men were. Then, having tied up the sleeping man, she went down the corridor to the occupied room. Lotte called her to say the three men were sitting at the table playing cards. They were all smoking and there were drinks on the table.

"Are there any weapons in sight?" Abby asked.

"Not that I can see." Lotte was not too certain.

"Lotte, is your gun in your hand, preferably cocked and safe?"

There was a pause of a few moments before the answer came. "It is now."

Abby opened the door and stepped into the room. Her Glock was in her hand out of sight. "Evening, boys. Having a good time, are we?" Her mask was up on top of her head and she smiled brightly. "Mr. Remington asked me to pop in and see that you boys have all you need."

There was a stunned silence as the three men looked up and took in the sight of the pretty girl in the coveralls standing front of them. One of the men started to stand up, reaching for something partly hidden by a pile of books and money.

Abby sighed and produced the Glock. "Two fingers. Put it in the centre if the table, with the pot."

The standing man carefully picked up the automatic and placed it in the centre of the table. With her gun Abby invited the other two to rise and produce their weapons. The one on the right did exactly that while the left hand man tried his luck. Collecting his weapon in his left hand, he started to turn. Abby shot him in the head, the silenced weapon bucked in her hand and immediately returned to cover the other two. He dropped on the spot. The men froze, shocked.

"Now, please come out into the centre of the room where we can see you. Good. Now drop your pants and kick them away from you."

The pair complied revealing the ankle holstered guns both carried.

Abby motioned to the weapons and they were carefully placed on the table with the others. To the taller of the men she pointed at the dead man. "Please relieve him of his weapons."

The man removed the Browning automatic from the dead man's clenched hand, and the gun from his ankle holster. With all the weapons accounted for, Abby pulled her mask down and produced her aerosol. "Good night, gentlemen!" She said, as she sprayed the pair with the anaesthetic.

"Come in, Lotte. We'll join the others."

Donny and Tom came down with their prisoner, an angry scrawny little man with swarthy complexion and several days' growth of dark beard. His thick, wild black hair was uncombed.

"It took longer than we thought," Tom said. "We had to subdue his bedmate."

"And get him dressed. It would not have been right to bring him down in his sleeping gear." Donny commented, "We also had to send his companion back to sleep."

Abby shrugged and Lotte giggled. "So we leave now. Yes?"

"I'm afraid not yet." Abby said. Now we search for papers, evidence etc. Let's get on with it."

Donny locked the prisoner to the dead man, at wrist and ankle, and left him with Lotte. The others spread through the house searching through for papers. In the agents' rest room the cabinet produced official CIA papers, detailing instructions for the protection and support of the asset. No names given.

The group, with prisoner then moved to the gate house. The suspicious keeper succumbed to the ether spray, just like the others. They were all there when the van returned. It hooted. Tom looked to the others and pressed the button to open the gates. As the van moved forward Donny stepped out with the clipboard. The driver did not even look up. He reached for the clipboard, looking disgusted. The ether spray gushed in his face. His companion reached for his weapon. But his dose of gas was too much. Like the driver he collapsed.

The van had no cargo except a stack of eight pizza boxes with a variety of pizzas. The intruders took the wallets and weapons. As an afterthought they took the pizzas as well.

***

In the Campanile the room was crowded, the atmosphere cheerful as they waited for Jonathon and his collection team.

When he arrived he took one look at the prisoner, and nodded. "Good. Any documents or other evidence?"

The bag of papers was passed over. To the relief of the four young people the collection party left them to themselves. Tom and Lotte got a room at the hotel, rather than returning to the hostel where they had checked-in earlier. Abby rang the hostel and arranged to have them keep the three packs until the next day, telling them they were crashing at friends for the night.

***

As they lay in companionable silence later that night, Donny sat up and spoke. "I am sorry that the man Remington was not there today. I have this feeling in my bones that we will be hearing from him sooner rather than later."

"You really think so? With what we know, I should have thought he would be fading back into the woodwork, for a while at least. Certainly until the dust settles. This business must cause him embarrassment, surely?"

"I wouldn't bank on it. We have encountered the CIA before. They are not famous for taking advice nor are they known for tact. Running drugs or private wars. Yes, that's way up the list. Forgetting their own mistakes. Yes again. Forgiving whistleblowers and interference from other agencies, private individuals etc. No. So you see, I do not believe we are done with them yet. I will be surprised if our friend, Oskar, stays in custody more than 24 hours."

"Ah. So that's the way the wind blows. What's next?"

"Nothing at present. We are stuck waiting for the shoe to drop. To react we will need information

and with Jonathon being so close mouthed......."
He shrugged.

"We just go back to La Rochelle and make for
Malta then?"

Donny lay down again. "It's a plan. Let's get
some sleep."

Abby rolled over beside him "We can sleep
later." She said.

***

They returned to La Rochelle to find their boats
unharmed.

Will and Mary had decided to cruise to Gibraltar to lie up over the winter. Will regarded the alteration to their plans as a move in the right direction. Maybe they would move on to the Mediterranean proper afterwards. Suddenly Will was getting
restless and a little anxious over Mary and Lotte.
The recent events were challenging. He did not like
the attack on his family.

It was in company that the two boats sailed. By
agreement they decided to stay together for the voyage. Having been advised of the previous intervention of the *Stroller*, Donny suggested that two
would be more difficult to intercept than one.

Will suggested that there was no longer any
reason for them to be intercepted them as the delivery had been made.

Donny looked at him keenly. "Commander, we
are all members of the club, Lotte, Tom, Mary and

us. I remind you there is no need to keep things from any of us. You know how things work in our business. If you lose one you suck it up, but you get your own back as soon as the opportunity offers." The chances are that Peter Speight will know that you are sailing to Gibraltar, and what time you are leaving. The important thing is you cannot afford to let your guard down. It isn't only you. As things are, you do have a right bunch of ruffians sailing with you. That means firepower, but he knows that already from the first clash. We are going that way anyway, so sailing in concert makes sense."

"Okay. I have got the message. I just felt guilty about holding you both up, especially after the latest operation in Paris. I just thought that I should have done my job properly. Then it would not have been needed."

Abby smiled. "Will, that operation was dreamed up by Jonathon. The reason was nothing to do with you, I'm afraid. We went for and caught Oskar Renko. The reason you were not told was the old story of 'need to know'."

In the Bay of Biscay the waters are seldom calm, and on sailing day they were lively without being excessively rough. Both of the craft were good sailors and they were able to make good progress reaching out towards the wide Atlantic. Clearing Cape Finisterre was their first objective. With a north-easterly wind the two craft made quick time and, as luck would have it, there was no sign of any interference with their progress. By the time they changed course to parallel the Iberian peninsula the settled weather was beginning to change. The gathering clouds fraying round the edges were depositing rain carried by the wind, making the steering uncomfortable on both craft. It made sense to shorten sail as the wind was predicted to increase during the night. For the ketch, the storm jib and what Donny called a hankie on the mizzen, the *Swallow* managed well enough. For the *Speedwell* it was more or less the same situation with the same answer, storm jib, reefed mizzen. Both kept in touch carrying lights, and by radar.

They were rounding Cape Trafalgar when the message came from Jonathon. "Oskar Renko released to US custody am today. Watch your backs. No progress on Remington. No one is admitting he is one of their team."

***

It was fortuitous that the Commander was able to moor at the naval base. The reduction in the fleet due to cuts in expenditure meant that many of the berths traditionally occupied were vacant and there was room for the *Speedwell* to lie alongside. Donny sailed in to one of the marina temporary berths.

All six gathered at the Caleta hotel for dinner and a farewell party. They all stayed at the hotel that night.

The following morning they came back to earth with a bang. Donny and Abby returned to the marina in the morning. The gatekeeper greeted them. He said "Did your friend find you last night?"

"Friend! Did he give his name?"

"Why? No. He seemed to know who you were, mentioned you both."

Abby said, "What did he look like?"

"He was well dressed, an American I think."

"Did he go out to the boat?" Donny asked.

"Oh no, sir. I knew you were out. I never let strangers into the marina." The gatekeeper was definite and they had no difficulty in believing him.

As they were speaking, a car pulled up at the parking area serving the section where visiting boats were accommodated. A tall, suited, clean-cut looking man got out and walked towards the gate.

The gatekeeper smiled. "Here is the gentleman now, the man looking for you."

Donny thanked him and turned to meet their visitor. "I believe you were asking for us last night?"

"If you are Donald Weston and Abby Marshall, then I certainly was."

The gatekeeper opened the gate and left them to it.

"And you are?" Abby queried.

The man reached carefully into his pocket and withdrew a leather folder, He opened it revealing a gold badge, and an i/d card identifying him as James Beckett, FBI, Special agent "My name is Beckett, James Beckett FBI. I am looking into the whereabouts and activities of a man named Paul Remington, CIA agent in charge, Europe. I understand you may be able to assist me."

"Are you armed, Agent Beckett?" Donny asked politely.

Their visitor looked at them both steadily. "I am," he said quietly. He unbuttoned his jacket and opened the left side to reveal a glimpse of the holstered automatic. He released the cloth and re-buttoned his jacket.

"Why don't you join us on our boat, Mr Beckett? We will be more comfortable and we can discuss your mission over coffee."

Abby led the way to the *Swallow* and unlocked the hatch.

The scent of the brewing coffee soon overlaid the crisp perfume of the Beckett aftershave or deodorant. Abby was not sure which it was. She was sure that James Beckett was not an FBI agent. She was also aware that, though the FBI were responsible for the security at US Embassies, they were not permitted by law, to operate overtly outside the United States. Finally the perfume was a step too far. Agents operating in plain-clothes would only wear strong perfume as part of a cover. Drawing attention to oneself with loud clothes, odd facial hair or strong perfume was a definite no, no!

Once in the saloon Abby had gone to the stove to make coffee, Donny ushered their guest in and produced his Glock. "Weapon please, Mr Beckett, or whoever you are. Two fingers only."

The man turned and unbuttoned his jacket and lifted the weapon from his underarm holster. He placed it carefully on the table.

Abby turned from the stove, gun in hand, and stood while Donny frisked Beckett for other weapons. Then he indicated the bench seat beside the saloon table.

He picked up the surrendered gun with a pencil, sliding the end into the open barrel. Sniffing the barrel he turned to Beckett. "Who did you shoot, Mr. Beckett? Could it possibly have been James Beckett?"

The man started to rise but because of the table could not, trapped by the close proximity of the seat to the table. ""Now, listen. I can explain. I...."

The bullet came through the open hatch. It was very good shooting. The hatch was open to the sea. It meant that the shot had been fired from a passing boat, or a sniper from the sea wall, half-mile distant. A boat, passing, caused the ketch to rock the fenders squeaking at the pressure.

Beckett was looking bad. The spreading stain on his immaculate shirt was the only mark to be seen from the front.

Donny said, "Hang on. We'll get help."

Beckett shook his head. "Too late. Get that bastard Remington. He told me just a little acting job, so that he could photograph you both. Industriaa...." The eyes glazed, Beckett died.

Abby called from the deck. As soon as the bullet had hit Beckett, she had dashed through to the fore-hatch. With binoculars she searched the area offshore where the bullet must have originated. The departing power boat was the only possibility. The name on the stern was *Stroller,* though it could have been anything. Changing a name or covering it was easy. She took a picture with the camera integral with the binoculars, and then returned to the saloon.

"They made sure," Donny said, "The bullet was dum-dum or soft tipped. No exit wound!" He went through the man's jacket and pant's pocket's, piling the contents on the table top.

Abby picked up a billfold. There were two one-hundred dollar bills, plus local money, several business cards, two with photo i/d. Both the same man Beckett's picture, though the names were different. There was also a hand-bill from a theatre in Connecticut for 'The man who wasn't there.' Starring Michael Watson, the photo was of a younger version of Beckett. The date was 1996.

Abby looked at the dead man. "So it was a farewell performance, Michael Watson. This was the part you should not have accepted."

Donny dialled Jonathon on the coded number.

"What now?" Jonathon sounded pissed.

"We are in Gibraltar."

"Oh. It's you two. I know, someone called the Gibraltar Police saying there is a dead man on your boat."

"That's why we called. He was taken out by a sniper from, we believe, a power boat named *Stroller*. Any ideas?"

"Sit tight. I am in touch with the local police on the other line. They should be with you any minute."

Donny heard the sound of the sirens.

"I can hear them now." He said. "Wasn't *Stroller* the name of the boat that attacked the *Speedwell*?"

"Yes, it was. Deal with the police. They know you are ours. So there should be no problems." Jonathon rang off,

Chapter Six...Cat and Mouse.

The police in Gibraltar were rather aggressive despite Jonathon's reassurance. Donny and Abby were bundled into a police car and taken to the police headquarters. They had put their own weapons away. The only weapon on show was the one taken from Beckett's underarm holster. They spent the night in the cells.

The following day Will was there, pounding the counter, facing the Inspector in charge. His i/d for Naval Intelligence open on the counter. "Why were we not informed? This is a security matter. Nothing to do with the police, the standing orders state that security matters be passed to my department immediately."

"I was called by the CIA who advised me that there had been a shooting by known spies on the boat at the marina. The man used the proper code so the call had to be genuine. He said there would be proof of murder at the scene. The people involved were armed and dangerous."

"So you went off like bunch of cowboys, ignoring protocol on the word of a so-called CIA agent!"

"He was an agent. He knew the code word for yesterday!" The Inspector was frustrated and baffled.

"What now? Do they go to court?"

"No. There was a fired gun, but the only prints on it are the victim's. There was no powder on either prisoner's hands. The autopsy found a soft-nosed rifle round killed the man.

Will was not mollified. This had been a breach of protocol. Remington had played the system and might have got away with it if Donny and Abby not reacted as they did.

Donny and Abby appeared from the cell block at this time. They signed for their possessions, then demanded, and received, photocopies of the contents of the documents found on Beckett/Watson, the dead man.

Donny turned to the Inspector. "What part of this did you misunderstand, Inspector." He held up his warrant i/d, stating his membership of M16 with photograph. It called for the cooperation of all law enforcement officers.

"The CIA man said you had false identities."

"So you believed him, without checking with security? Thank you, Inspector. The man is clever and obviously plausible. Okay, Inspector. I can see you were doing your best in tricky circumstances. It's better dealing with it this way than to make an expensive error."

They left the Police headquarters with Will and returned to the boat to clear up.

There was not much mess. The police had been more concerned with the body and the weapon than the boat in general. They did find a second bullet, buried in the L-shaped end of the bench seat. It was next to a button in the upholstery and not easily seen. Abby had felt the rough edge when she leaned down to search for anything fallen down behind the seat squab.

She dug the bullet out, and held it up. "So they took two shots. I'm not really surprised. It was an incredible shot in any circumstances."

Will said ,"What happens now?"

Donny looked thoughtful. "We have to wait for Jonathon to get in touch. Meanwhile it's back to the night life of Gibraltar, I suppose."

***

On the *Stroller*, Peter Speight was arguing with the big American. Remington towered over him, but he was not overawed. "We funded you in this harebrained scheme. So far all we have seen are bodies. Have you any results to show for the outlay of our money?"

"Nothing comes too easy in this business. It will take time. Remember we have UNOCON to contend with!"

"Bollocks! You know as well as I do that was just a smoke screen for the real operation. I would prefer you actually concentrated on that, rather than bugger about playing games with your spook pals."

Remington looked at Peter Speight calculatingly, wondering how far he should allow this man to go before he killed him.

***

Natalie Speight watched him from across the room. She quite enjoyed having him around. Preoccupied with her own agenda, she enjoyed Paul Remington as a bed mate, but otherwise he could be rather boring. As for her father, well that was another issue. She had considered having Paul remove him, but decided to leave things until this latest exercise was worked out.

She smiled to herself, thinking of the way people treated her father. If they only knew what a complete animal he was. Her own experience was based on the introduction to her body demonstrated by her father. Reaching puberty for her was not a time of love and romance. It was an occasion of terror and pain. A series of intrusions by her father her mother had done nothing to prevent. She had miscarried at fifteen, and lost her capacity to produce children at the medical procedure that followed. From that time sex had become a weapon in the war between the sexes as she saw it.

When her mother had died, playing with a mixture of drugs and rough sex. Natalie had been pleased, served the bitch right.

Her father had indicated he would expect her to take her mother's place in his household and bed. The stiletto she had produced when he came to claim her after the funeral changed his attitude. She made it clear that any relations between them in future would be at her dictation, not his.

***

Oskar Renko studied her from his place at the desk in the corner of the saloon. He had already decided that he would possess her when he was ready. She was ruthless enough to make a suitable playmate for now anyway. There was no doubt in his mind that, apart from himself, she was the most dangerous person in the room.

The *Stroller* eased into her berth in Tangier. Renko sighed with relief. He was not altogether happy on the ocean. The thought of walking on solid ground was appealing.

He had been pleased with his marksmanship in shooting the dupe on the ketch. That had been a truly tricky shot. It had taken two shots but, even with the drag of the silencer, his aim had been true. He smiled and turned to Natalie, "Shall we take a stroll ashore while they play games?"

"Why not!" Natalie answered. "Let's leave them to it."

***

There was a base in Tangier for the group. Remington had a CIA house and Speight Industries had an apartment and an office here.

In the privacy of the apartment Oskar and Natalie indulged themselves in bed in what turned out to be a satisfying experience for them both. Neither was accustomed to the experience, both normally having to settle for less.

Oskar smiled to himself, his guess had been right. Natalie decided it was a good start. Both had already decided that, when the others had finally settled the arrangements for the coup, neither would live to enjoy the results.

***

For Donny and Abby, the call from Jonathon finally came through. "We are now getting to the real story behind the operation being driven by Remington and Renko. The operation is nothing to do with money. It's an assassination."

"Who are they after? Do we know?" Donny asked.

"We suspect it's the German Chancellor Hansie Krabbe."

Donny breathed out with a whoosh. "Krabbe! They are really after a prize. Mind you, with the sniper that got Beckett yesterday, anything is possible."

"Do we know where the *Stroller* finished up?" Abby asked.

"Spotted going into Tangier carrying three passengers. One woman, and two men. One of the men fits the description of Oskar Renko. I guess it's Peter and Natalie Speight. It appears that Oskar is the shooter. Our local man suspects that Remington will appear for a meeting.

"They have set up in the CIA house for the moment. Natalie will probably head for the nearest resort hotel. The house is pretty spartan."

"Do you want us to see if we can eliminate the threat? What do the cousins say about Oskar?"

"They are still covering for Remington. He must have some powerful friends in the agency. If you do think you can make a difference, don't take the boat. As tourists you would have a better chance of escaping attention."

Donny looked at Abby, the question in his raised eyebrow.

She nodded. "Let's take a look at least."

"We'll keep you in touch. Can we contact the local man?" Donny said hopefully.

"I'll leave it to him. I think he will contact you. I suggest you use the backpacker route. Stay in a hostel, eat on the street, but take gear for the posh places."

"Jonathon!" Abby interrupted. "We know what to do!"

"Oh, ah, sorry. I get carried away sometimes. I keep thinking of you as youngsters. Good luck and... oh, you know."

"Thanks, Jonathon. Goodbye!" Both called out.

Over the past years they had built up a good relationship with Jonathon. His attitude had always been that of favoured uncle, rather than boss. Given the friendship between Donny's father and Jonathon it was understandable.

***

The ferry was fairly crowded. The pair had elected to take a hire car across with them. They booked into the Ibis hotel in Tangier in advance, and expected to drive direct there when the ferry arrived. The local agent contacted them at the hotel. He was a rather swarthy young man, wearing Arab/western garb. He arrived at their room shortly after they did. His name was Michael Smith and he had established himself there in the travel business three years ago.

"What do you want to do about the group?"

Donny looked at the young man speculatively. "Do they know you here? I mean have you any overt links with our people in the Embassy?"

"No. I work outside the box. I have my own source of supply. I keep informed through coded transmissions through the travel agency and my coded cell phone."

"Well, we will be taking the shooter out, if we can." Donny said.

Michael Smith looked startled, "Taking him out?"

Abby smiled grimly. "Oskar Renko has killed more innocent people than any other individual terrorist; as far as admitted killings are concerned, that is. He has targeted a European leader we believe. So he must be stopped."

Smith was still looking shocked, but it seemed more at thought of the pretty girl in front of him talking so calmly about taking a killer out, killing someone!

Smith got out the map of the city which he had brought with him and showed them the location of the house where the opposition was based. "I have a watcher on site keeping an eye on the house," he said. "She should be able to tell at any time how many are in or out."

"Contact?" Abby asked.

"By cell phone, basically."

"Right. That makes sense. So we wait?"

Smith nodded. "Yes. Waiting for things to happen seems to be what this business is all about." He looked at Abby. "What got you into this business?"

Abby smiled. "Donny and I were delivering his Dad's boat to France. We bumped into trouble with smuggling. They pushed and tried to kill us, so we killed them. The rest is history."

Smith looked at Donny who shrugged and said, "Just about sums it up."

The cell phone rang, the discussion stopped while Smith answered the call.

After a few words the call finished. Smith turned to the others and said, "All three are in the house, Oskar, Natalie and Peter."

***

The car stopped on the side of the road. The two people left it, hurrying toward the market place. When the man returned and got into the car he was dressed in Arab garb. He drove off, and in the next street, picked up a second person also in Arab dress. The car then made a dash for the port area. There, parked among the many other cars, the two Arabs abandoned it.

The area around the safe house was busy with vehicles coming and going. There were plenty of people moving about, some standing gossiping and smoking. The two extra people made no real impact on the scene.

The house was silent, no sign of life. The hope that they would get a sight of their target was fading with the light.

The situation changed dramatically. When the door opened all three occupants came out, arguing. Donny shouted and all three stopped to look. Abby shot Oskar through his forehead. The back of his skull exploded, splattering Natalie with its contents.

There was a sudden silence finally broken by the scream of frustration and disgust from Natalie.

The second shot took Peter in the shoulder, low, clipping his lung and exiting through his scapula. He fell, crumpling to the ground spitting blood. Natalie dived back into the house, ignoring the two downed men.

The people outside the area scattered in panic. From the house Natalie looked through the monitors carrying a view from all the concealed cameras. There was no sign of the shooter. The two men on the ground, one moving, the other still, were isolated. None of the people in the area was approaching the wounded man to give aid. In the end Natalie went to the door and opened it. She dashed out to her wounded father and threw herself down at his side, away from the direction from which the shots had originated. Her wounded father was conscious and he smiled grimly. His daughter was no fool. Anyone still shooting would have to shoot through him to get to her. He had trained her well.

"Right. Get me out of here. If they were going to shoot you, they would have turned me into a colander by now."

She thought for a moment and then rose to her feet and grabbed him by the shoulders, dragging at his wounded side as well as the unhurt.

Her father groaned aloud, but gritted his teeth and suffered, as she hauled him through the front door into the hall.

"Call the emergency number. Get a doctor!" Her father gritted through the pain. "Tell that yank, Remington, to get his arse in gear. Or his whole scheme will be finished before it starts."

Natalie called the private number and gave the bad news. Then she shoved a towel against her father's back and a second at the entry wound. "I can take the shot!" She said, "I'm as good as Oskar was any day."

Peter looked at her. "Oskar was expendable," he said. It was the nearest thing to a term of endearment she had heard from him for years.

***

Paul Remington arrived at the house with three other agents and the doctor. Between them they managed to get Peter Speight into a bed. The doctor then went to work on him while Remington joined Natalie to discuss what had happened that morning.

"The loss of Oskar is bad news for us, though the other agencies will be pleased. He has been on their wanted list for years."

"Why did you bother with him in the first place?" Natalie asked.

"Basically, he would have been the ideal candidate for the shooting. We could have dumped him to kept the pressure off us He was the perfect patsy, taking all the blame and keeping us clean."

"I suggested that I could take the shot. I shoot as well as Oskar did. Father said 'no' and I presume he was talking about the same thing that you are. Oskar would have been there to take the blame if necessary for the operation. Were you going to shoot him in valiant defence of the target?" Even in the privacy of the safe house she would not use the name.

Remington looked at Natalie sharply. There was more to this young lady than met the eye. "You are quite right. That would have been the plan. Now we will have to make alternative arrangements."

She smiled grimly. "The background arrangements can remain in place. All that really needs to be done is to find the, how shall I put it, culprit, just to make it clear who planned the assassination."

"You seemed to have worked that out pretty well. So what happens now?" Remington decided to see what she had in her mind.

Natalie could feel the excitement building in her mind, as she contemplated the thrill of killing at a distance, anonymously. It was something that had not up to now occurred to her. But now the idea thrilled her. She could feel her body reacting, causing her to shift in her seat with her sexual reaction to the prospect of the killing. She looked at Remington. "I have someone in mind to take over the role of Oskar, after I have done the shooting." Her hand went to Paul Remington's face. She stroked his cheek, looking into his eyes and leaning toward him. "But we have time for that later. Her fingers strayed to his shirt front and she undid one button. She ran her nail down through the hair of the exposed section of his bared chest. It was the sexiest thing that Remington had experienced for nearly a year. His hands reached out to the buttons of her blouse.

In the kitchen of the house the doctor reported to Remington that Peter Speight would live, but that it would be weeks before his wound would allow him full mobility of his arm and shoulder. The doctor left, leaving a pack of dressings, painkillers and antibiotics for the patient.

Remington put the coffee pot on the stove and was joined by Natalie who was now wearing a silk dressing gown loosely tied at the waist.

"Your father will recover in time." Paul Remington said. "I'll ship him back to UK. Do you want to go with him?"

Natalie shook her head. "No. He has plenty of help at home. I'll stay and keep involved if you don't mind." She smiled and pulled the tie round her waist. As the gown opened revealing her naked body, she said, "You won't mind, will you?"

He turned and pushed down the jogging pants he was wearing, then moved her back across the kitchen table. "I'll manage," he murmured.

Chapter seven...Munich-Strasbourg

Two weeks and getting nowhere, Tom and Lotte joined Donny on the veranda of the chalet. "Where are we now then?" Lotte asked.

She and Tom had just arrived at Oetz in Tyrol on the Orient Express. Not, she would have hastened to say, on the luxury gin palace but on the standard train.

Donny smiled. "Well, we have good news and bad news. The good is that Oskar was in fact removed from the equation in Tangier. Peter Speight got a wound in his shoulder and is hors de combat for the next few weeks at least. Natalie survived unscathed apparently. She is currently still with Remington, somewhere in Germany. Jonathon has his spies out as we speak. We are concerned with the conference of the EU leaders and the special meetings between Germany, France and UK. The Russian premier will be in the offing for the celebrations of the end of WW11."

"Who is the target?" Tom asked. "Do we know yet?"

Abby walked in from the kitchen in time to field his question. "Hansie Krabbe is favourite, though Vladimir Schukov, the Russian Premier comes a close second."

"Who are these people? What is it they are trying to achieve?"

Donny came in again. "Best guess so far is, the Islamic faction, any combination of Muslim alphabet soup, including Al Qaeda. It does seem that the smokescreen about UNOCON was just that. A screen to cover up their real purpose, whatever that is. What they are aiming to get out of it? Your guess is as good as mine."

The four people settled down for the evening, chatting to bring themselves up to date. They had gone their separate ways after Gibraltar, though Tom and Lotte had elected to leave the schooner at Malta, and come to join Donny and Abby here in Austria.

Will and Mary had left the schooner in Malta and grabbed a lift on a westbound yacht calling at Gibraltar. Their purpose was to pick up *Swallow,* Donny and Abby's ketch, and deliver it to Malta for them, they having been diverted to Tangier. The ketch had been booked into the yard at Valetta, so they would rejoin the *Speedwell* when they arrived with the ketch.

In Oetz, the four young people went skiing. As Abby pointed out, it was better to keep fit rather than to hang about and grow fat. All carried cell phones so they could be in touch wherever they were.

Donny was halfway down the mountain when his cell bleeped. He left it until he reached the foot of the run before he answered. Naturally, he had to call Jonathon back. Jonathon had moved on and was not immediately available. It was early evening when they finally made contact.

"You will need to pack up and join us in Strasbourg. Do you know where your friends are, as we have decided they can be of use to the department?"

"Tom and Lotte are with us here in Oetz. We will bring them along with us. Do you need anything else?"

"No, but I have a message from Will and Mary. They say they have picked up the *Swallow* and are en route to Valetta, whatever that means."

"If that's all, we'll get moving tomorrow, on the early train from Munich. We should be with you by tomorrow night."

The hire car was deposited at the hauptbahnhof in Munich the following morning. The four friends boarded the TGV for the journey of just under four hours to Strasbourg. Abby promptly went to sleep, having risen, as she put it, at the crack of dawn. The train raced smoothly across the Bavarian countryside and the other three talked quietly while Abby slept. Lotte gave up the battle and joined Abby, while the two men discussed their options quietly.

Donny asked Tom what he felt about Jonathon's assumptions.

"I think, in this instance, Lotte and I are both willing to pull our weight sorting this problem out. But I also think it will depend on what happens in this current situation. Personally, I think we will be alright, possibly happy to continue, like yourselves. But, as I have said, let's wait and see."

Donny smiled quietly. "I watched you during the episode in La Rochelle. I don't have any doubts. But, as you say, we'll wait and see."

Both relaxed back and watched the scenery fly past the windows. Donny noticed that one of the faces reflected in the window seemed very interested in the group. He had not seen the man before, so he must have entered the carriage after the train started moving. He studied the man in the reflection noting the dark hair and the aquiline nose. It was not possible to see how big he was though Donny did get the impression of wide shoulders and muscular body. The man was wearing a sweater with a pattern of skiers in a band around it at chest level. Over the next few miles he managed to visit the rest room, and work out that the sweater man had a partner at the other end of the carriage.

Returning to his seat, he passed on the information to Tom who hauled up his laptop case and retrieved his laptop. At the same time he slipped the

Walther PPK out of the case and into the waistband of his chinos.

Donny was intrigued by the appearance of followers so quickly. How did they know that they would be travelling to Strasbourg from Munich?

Abby came up with, "If either Lotte or Tom had used their cell phones…Oh blast! They do not have to use their cell phones, all they had to do was carry them. We are dealing CIA, it has to be part of their routine to have a way of tracking locations by known cell numbers." She turned to Tom and Lotte who was wide awake once more. "When we reach Strasbourg, Donny and I will drop off the map. Our cell phones are codex and it would take an act of Congress for the US President to get permission to track us. You two get off the train at Stuttgart. Go straight out of the station. Dump your cell phones on some passing truck or bus. You can get others at any of the phone outlets. I suggest you get a hire car and drive to meet us in Strasbourg. We'll meet at the posh bridge. You know the one, Donny, the 'Pont des Deux Rives' It crosses the Rhine into Kehl in Germany. I'm pretty sure it's a footbridge, so we should be able to spot followers!"

"Sounds good to me. OK with you, Lotte?" Tom asked.

Lotte nodded and with a grin said, "And I thought that James Bond stuff was all story book spy stuff. I feel as if we are playing a game here."

She looked around at the other three serious faces. "It isn't a game, is it? Its real guns, real bullets, real bodies! I did know, but I still have to pinch myself sometimes just to make sure." She sat back serious-faced. As youngest of the four and the most un-worldly as yet, the other three did understand. Lotte would be fine and with Tom beside her, the other two had no doubts.

As the train pulled into Stuttgart hauptbahnhof, passengers started to move about and all four got off the train to stretch their legs. There were many people milling about the platform. The train was only there for a few minutes. As the passengers started to cram themselves back through the doors, Abby was able to see Tom and Lotte making their separate ways through the barriers.

In the carriage once more, the places occupied by Lotte and Tom were taken by an elderly pair of expatriates from USA, returning to visit the land of their youth. The Michigan couple from Coldwater, lecturers at the University of Michigan, were tour-ing Europe and UK over the next two months. Both were recovering from the entertainment they had received in Munich. As they poured out their recol-lections of the night before, Donny looked at the followers; the nearest one was still in place. It was not until later that the second man appeared, having probably searched the train for the others. Donny was not happy. He blamed himself for the easy way the opposition had picked them up in the first place.

Abby grinned at him as he settled down once more. "They think they have been tricked! Sorry. They know they've been tricked."

Donny said, "They should not have known we were here in the first place. That was my fault. I know about tracking cell phones. I should have realised and warned Tom when they rejoined us."

Abby looked concerned and leaned forward. "It is not your fault. I am here too. I know about these things as well. We are a partnership. We know how things work. If something goes wrong, and you know very well things will go wrong, it's what you do about it that counts. We have done all we can. So we live with it. If something comes out of it we deal with it. Right?"

"Beautifully put!" Donny answered with a smile. He sat back feeling better. That's what often happened between them. He wondered sometimes what he would do without her. Then he fell asleep.

***

As the train approached Strasbourg, Donny woke to find the people all around them stirring and collecting their things for when the train finally stopped.

Donny realised that Abby was missing, and saw her coming into the carriage behind the watcher. He was just lifting his cell phone to his ear as Abby smacked him round the face with a full roundhouse swing of her arm. "Pervert!" She shouted. "Keep your filthy hands to yourself!"

The watcher lost his cell phone which landed on the floor and slid almost to Donny's feet. While the attention of the crowd was centred on the unfolding drama created by Abby, he slid it in his pocket.

Meanwhile two burly young men were gripping the watcher, who was protesting violently as Abby lifted her short skirt to show the audience where the man had groped her. The performance gave a spectacular view of her lace-trimmed white panties. This distracted the male members of the audience' as her other hand lifted the unfortunate watcher's man-bag from the table in the flurry of distractions. Dropping her skirt once more she flounced hack to Donny and her seat, leaving the escalating disturbance to the two German lads who were not allowing the watcher to take any further part in the proceedings.

The watcher did manage to get loose and ran down the aisle towards his partner at the other end of the carriage. He was tripped and fell sprawling on the way and three men dropped on him. His partner disappeared out of the far door, the train having halted by now.

Donny and Abby left in time to see the head of the partner through the bobbing heads of the other passengers. They were able to keep him in sight as he passed through the barrier and saw his contact. The two men spoke briefly and split-up. They carried on following the new contact. They lost him in the traffic outside the station.

Abby grabbed a cab and they went to the rendezvous, beside the Rhine. On a seat on their own, Abby showed Donny the bag she had snatched from the watcher during the debacle on the train. Between them they ran through the contents. There was a sealed envelope with the name, Walther Grasse, written in ball point across the face. While Abby went through the wallet, Donny opened the envelope. Inside there was an American Express credit card and a Visa debit card, a note taped with them gave the pass codes for them both. The note was brief, written in German. Donny translated it aloud for Abby to hear. *Do not exceed 2,000 Euro's on the American Express. The Visa is open, use what you have to.* The letter R was scrawled under the note. "I presume we are looking at largesse on the account of CIA, courtesy of Paul Remington." Donny said dryly.

"They were not short of money." Abby commented producing a wad of Euro's from the wallet. "It appears Walther Grasse was a trusted member of the organisation!"

"Could you find anything else of interest in there?" Donny enquired.

"Two condoms and an inhaler, the rest we have seen. What's next?"

Donny smiled wickedly. "The nearest ATM, I think. Then some shopping would be fun."

"You wouldn't?"

"I would. Those two characters were not trailing us to offer assistance. You can be sure that we were scheduled for the chop. Let's go. I'm sure there will be an ATM in the building over there." Donny pointed to the park admin building, where there was a restaurant and shop.

"What about Tom and Lotte?"

"They will be here soon, I grant. But if we get the money before the cards are cancelled, they can help us spend it. Are you with me?"

With a laugh, Abby started toward the buildings, calling, "What are you waiting for? Come on, before they guess what we are up to."

They were back at the agreed meeting point before Tom and Lotte arrived. Having found four machines they had drawn out the maximum from each machine using both cards. The booty amounted to enough to make an interesting amount of cash for the girls to splash in the upmarket boutiques of the parliamentary capital of Europe.

Lotte, as was her habit, was immediately curious about the Parliament. "I thought Brussels was the capital of Europe. "What is going on here?"

Tom started to explain but Abby broke in. "Europe had a parliament here and an HQ in Brussels. The fact is that the EU is supposedly governed from here and administered from Brussels. In truth, Brussels seems to dictate what happens in the EU. The politicians in this case appear to be so well paid, that they don't wish to upset the apple cart by interfering with the decisions of the civil service which is, of course, Brussels. We are therefore the only Democratic group of nations to be ruled by the appointed civil service, as opposed to the elected politicians."

"But that is wrong. How do they get away with it?" Lotte said.

"As I explained money talks. Just like the Mafia. Pay them enough and they leave you alone"

Lotte looked around the group in amazement, "But......" She realised from the faces around her that Abby was serious.

"Come on, you lot. Let's splash the cash. We can get down to the serious business this evening when we meet the boss man."

***

The meeting with Jonathon in the Campanile Hotel that evening established the belief that the real target for assassination would be Hansie Krabbe, the German Chancellor.

"Why not Vladimir Schukov. Surely he would be much higher profile?" Tom asked.

"Because we are now convinced that Schukov is bankrolling this operation." Jonathon looked serious.

"Remington has gone over then?" Donny asked.

"This is strictly for cash. I see no evidence of Remington defecting. What I can see is the US Government eventually paying through the nose for keeping the peace after a successful assassination. That brings me to the point of our business, stopping the assassin!"

"Do we know who the assassin is?" Lotte asked.

"We now know it is not Oskar Renko." Jonathon answered. "At the moment there is no sign that Remington is actually trying to replace Oskar, so it looks as if an alternative is already available."

Lotte shocked them all. "It will be Natalie. She is a crack shot. It's just the sort of thing that vicious bitch would enjoy."

"Natalie Speight? You must be joking." Tom said.

The others said nothing, not really knowing who Natalie was.

Jonathon was quiet for a moment then he said slowly, "You could be right. As you say she is a crack shot with a rifle, if she has the nerve. 'The only thing that would be needed then is a victim to take the blame."

"Two things about Natalie you should know." Lotte had their attention now. "Natalie is the original sadist. Those she hates need to stay well clear of her. Reggie Swan, her best friend and equal shit, if you'll pardon the French, fell out with our Natalie. Reggie finished up with two broken legs when Natalie accidently smashed her up against the garage door with daddy's Jaguar. It has taken two years for her to recover. So yes, she has the nature to do the job. I presume Oskar was lined up to take the blame. That means that she will have her eyes on one of us for the purpose. That would be a typical Natalie answer. From the sound of it, that would suit Remington as well. For me, I think the blame should be laid at the feet of the originator of this little incident, especially if it is that grubby little crook Schukov." Lotte's remarks were followed by silence as the rest of the group considered what she had put forward.

Jonathon broke the silence. "What Lotte says about Natalie is chilling, I know. But in fact we have to work out our own program to make sure that we forestall any attempt to assassinate anyone at the summit conference. We know some of the people involved. Our problem is that the opposition has a right to be on site and we don't. CIA officials have not blacklisted Remington. They do not trust M16 in this matter and certainly will be well miffed at the death of Oskar Renko. They are definitely complicit in this shooting on the basis that they would have had complete deniability with Oskar involved. If they, as Lotte suggests, could frame one of us, they will be quite happy. The point being, that it is only Remington who is aware that the origin of this job is the Russian. His US bosses are being duped into allowing this killing because it would get rid of an embarrassment in Europe and a notorious terrorist at the same time."

"Someone mentioned that this may well be a cover for an even more devious operation to get rid of the Russian Premier." Donny reminded them. "What is the possibility that Remington is stringing everyone along?"

Jonathon pondered that comment for a few moments before eventually saying, "We could go on like this forever. We will need to concentrate on the actual shooting, I think. Unless we get hold of one of the inside men, the rest is academic. This is the way I see it. We cover Natalie Speight and find any fall-back situation they may have created. I have in mind an alternate shooter. I do not know of any in his present team, but, having said that, I did not know of Natalie until now. With that in mind we have two objectives. One to keep tabs on Natalie, the other to prevent any attempt to incriminate one of us. Keep your teams. Work together. And under no circumstances allow the opposition to isolate one of you. I will get the office to liaise with us from the security point of view. Are we all clear? "

They all nodded as his eyes swept round the group. "You are all known to our side, but may not be by theirs. They are checked in at the Holiday Inn in the town centre, so we have a starting place."

Jonathon left at that point, the four sat around the room working at the problem individually. Eventually, Abby stood up and, smoothing out the creases in her skirt, she said, "I am hungry. Anyone else interested?"

The others all perked up at this suggestion and the four went down to the restaurant to eat.

Chapter eight...Risky business

The difficulty of surveillance, when you are known to your subjects, is that fact that you are known. Despite the popular notion that beards, moustaches and wigs are the answer, the true art of disguise is minimal use of these items, and maximum use of body image. Stance, attitude and body language are the major points of recognition, with alteration to hair style, colour, glasses, and clothes to suit. Donny and Abby were now checked in at the Holiday Inn and keeping an eye on the Remington group with that in view. The blond-haired Lotte and Tom, looking like a pair of Nordic backpackers, were based still at the Campanile. But, with the acquisition of a VW Camper van, they were able to use a local car park and stay in the vicinity. Watching the comings and goings of the CIA party was illuminating and it was becoming increasingly evident that the Russians had an interest in whatever they were planning. The log of people entering and leaving the suit of rooms occupied by the Remington party showed the regular attendance of two major Russian members of the FSB. The replacement for the former KGB Major Abramovich and Captain

Carla Oblamov appeared on a regular basis, the Captain usually dressed in tee shirts and jeans and the Major in a lounge suit. Neither stayed more than two hours at any time, and on all occasions, the known members of the Remington team were present.

Remington himself appeared frequently, and Natalie stayed there most of the time. The other member of the group was a stranger to them all. Though he spoke with an American accent, Tom thought he was European, perhaps German, about 35 years, fresh-faced with a scar on his right cheek. The brown hair looked natural, but Tom guessed it was a well-made wig. The stranger they learned, was named Aaron Albrecht, though the four watchers doubted if the name was any more genuine than the wig he wore. He had the look of a killer. The innocent look was deceptive. His eyes had the stony dead look that indicated a complete lack of interest in the affairs of others, the frequent smiles never quite making it to his eyes.

The arrival of two 'suits', men dressed in Armani with underarm rigs that shouted Agency employees, created a relief from the boring round of inactivity for the watchers.

They arrived in a hired car and brought only briefcases with them, so they were obviously only visiting. They sent Aaron out to their car to retrieve what appeared to be a long black instrument case from the trunk. When they re-appeared the case stayed in the suite.

Donny made an on the spot decision. "Let's take those two and wring them out." He left his place and walked out to the car parked beside the hotel, Abby close behind but not convinced.

Abby, breathless, argued, "If they are missed there will be a complete change around. Remington will realise we are watching him."

"My guess is that they are visiting from HQ, and therefore do not appear above the radar. They will not be associated with Remington except at the highest level." He started the BMW they were using and drew out of the car park as the visitor's Mercedes drove into the traffic. They slipped into the stream of traffic two cars behind the Mercedes.

Abby shrugged. They were committed now. She called and told Tom and Lotte what was happening and that they were on their own, then produced her Glock, cocked it and set the safety. Donny leaned forward and she performed the same routine with his, slipping it carefully back into his waistband. "Any ideas on where they might be going?" She asked.

"I guess the Airport, though they could be going into Germany." They drove down the Rue-des-Mouettes. The Mercedes ahead indicated turning right under the railway.

"It's the airport." Donny said. He grunted with satisfaction as the Mercedes turned and slowed after the railway bridge, the driver unsure of the direction looking for the turnoff to the airport.

"He is going towards the Flying club entrance. They must have a private aircraft." He speeded up. As the Mercedes turned left he also turned and overtook the other car. They shot off down the Rue des Corps de Garde, quickly gaining the wooded section to the north of the airfield. He slowed up and thought for a few moments. There was not much traffic, most of the airfield traffic going into the main entrance where the commercial traffic was handled.

"We will go direct to the Aero club base and take the chance," he decided. "Okay with you?"

Abby grinned. "You are asking me. James Bond is asking Miss Moneypenny? Get on with it, Shames," Abby used her Sean Connery voice. "There will not be much time otherwise."

Donny laughed and using his Sean Connery voice answered. "Very well, Moneypenny. We'll do it my way." Ramming his foot on the accelerator, the BMW leaped down the road, turning right down past the Parachute training school to the club area where several light aircraft were parked. Among them was a small, twin jet executive aircraft with the airdoor open and integral steps deployed.

"That will be our target, I guess." Abby indicated. Donny drew into the shadow of the far side of the building, out of sight of the aircraft and they leapt out. The Mercedes was not yet in sight so they ran together over to the open door of the aircraft. Donny dashed through the door, straight into the arms of the woman straightening the magazines on the small table between the two armchairs in the cabin. Abby squeezed past him and went to the pilot's section where the pilot appeared to be imitating an ostrich head down in the well in front of the co-pilots seat. "Where did that bloody pen go?" The pad awaiting a signature lay on the seat. Under the edge Abby could see the tip of the lost pen. She leaned forward and picked it up. "Is this what you were looking for?" She said sweetly. The pilot reared up in surprise and banged his head against the dashboard. "Bugger!" He said with feeling. "I hate these little bastard planes. Why couldn't they use the Citation, or the Lear even." He suddenly realised that it was not the hostess he was addressing, a point reinforced by the Glock pressed into his cheek.

His companion had been thrust into one of the armchairs and was firmly strapped in with both seatbelt and her uniform jacket, now rather torn, acting as gag. The pilot found his hands caught together behind his seat, tied in place with his seat belt and the sleeve lining of his jacket. The other sleeve provided the gag.

Abby sat in the co-pilot's seat out of sight of the cabin. Donny occupied the other armchair.

The Mercedes drew up outside. The two men boarded, briefcases in hand, chatting together. They suddenly realised that there was something wrong.

"Come right in, gentlemen." Donny said politely. He directed the two men to the other two seats and made then place their briefcases on the table. "Now, one at a time please, two fingers only place the guns on the table."

With a shrug, the first man took out the Colt from his underarm rig. The other did the same. Donny removed both guns. Neither was carrying an ankle gun.

"Wallets, please?"

Both produced billfolds. As he looked at the first, he heard Abby say. "Don't even think about it."

He glanced up in amusement, "She hates disobedience," he said brightly. The shield in the first wallet was issued to Gordon Meadows, CIA Agent in Charge, Euro-Administration, Langley.

The other was similar, only he was apparently a foot soldier, his warrant stating he was merely Special Agent, Michael Roth. CIA.

"So, gentlemen. Please explain your business in Strasbourg?"

"Fuck off!" The senior agent answered. "You will regret this interference in US affairs."

"You will be kind enough to explain why you have just visited a cell of three terrorists, and delivered a sniper rifle to them. You will understand that I shall have no compunction in shooting you both, with full justification in the circumstances. If you can produce your authorised credentials as members of the security team in operation for the Euro summit that is about to commence, then I will be happy to apologise for your detention. The fact that you are carrying concealed weapons unlawfully, in a country friendly to the United States, may cause your Government some embarrassment. The presence of the sniper rifle will probably add up to life imprisonment for you both.

The special agent squirmed in his seat. "Come on, now. Who are you to threaten us like this? M16, French Security? I don't think so. So who?"

"I'm the one with the gun," Donny answered. He slammed the butt of the gun on the agent's knee.

The agent howled in pain, so Donny clouted him round the head with his gun hand, and man slumped in his seat, dazed and temporarily out of it.

Donny turned to the other man. His face had acquired pallor. It seemed he was no longer accustomed to the rough and tumble of an agent's life, if in fact he ever had been. To Donny he looked as though he had spent his life in an office, giving orders and expecting them to be obeyed.

"Now, look here, whoever you are. My government will not tolerate any interference with her representatives."

"I would be extremely surprised if the US government will publicly back an operation by their representatives to assassinate the head of a friendly nation, especially when it is revealed that they are acting at the behest of the Russian Premier. I have this vision of the US President bowing his head at the funeral of the friendly martyr, vowing the full force of the US descending on those involved in the foul deed. Whatever else, I also do not think your own boss realises that Remington has gone rogue. He has already compromised the US by taking on Oskar Renko, the man originally scheduled to perform the shooting, and, incidentally, to take the blame. His current shooter is a British woman who fondly expects to implicate someone else in the operation. She is certainly unaware of the fact that she herself will be the scapegoat in the matter."

Meadows blanched, his face paler than ever at the revelation of the matter which he had only been told was a standard, non-political wet job. He was, as Donny had suspected, a man who was normally employed in the office in an administrative role. His orders to make the delivery of the weapon had come out of the blue. He had allowed his imagination full reign, seeing himself as one of his heroes, dashing across the world to deliver essential equipment to agents in the field. The reason for the need for the weapon had made little impact on him. It had been enough that he was trusted to do such a task rather than leaving it to Roth, who certainly could have done the job. It was beginning to dawn on him that Colonel North had undertaken work for impeccable reasons and with the same dedication had unknowingly dug his own grave. The picture of a low level agent signing for the $20.000 sniper rifle, and delivering it, did not have the same cachet as that of a Senior Agent in Charge performing the same function.

He spoke slowly, "I do not know what you are talking about. I know nothing of assassination of a friendly head of state, or deals with the Russian Premier. It cannot be true."

Donny looked at him beginning to feel sorry for him. He well knew the sinking feeling that the unfortunate Meadows was getting, the realisation that he was being set up by his own people to cover the back of someone more important to the agency.

"Why would they do this to me? t cannot be true!"

"Sadly, Mr Meadows. I have no reason to make this up. You have been judged expendable by your own agency. Everything I have told you is absolutely true and I am charged with preventing it from happening."

"But my wife is a Deputy Director in the Agency. She would not allow them to frame me like this."

"Who briefed you for this job?"

"Why? My wife actually," said Meadows with relief . So you must be wrong. She would not be involved with any plot...like...that." His voice slowed down as he reached the end of his denial. "Would she?"

"You tell me, Mr Meadows. When did you last discuss agency affairs in detail?"

"We never talk about them. She does her work at home in her own bedroom."

"You don't sleep together then?"

Well, no. We married conveniently. I am not comfortable with women. Nor is she with men."

"Ah, I see." Donny dropped his eyes.

"What does that mean? Ah! What are you implying?"

"If your marriage is one of convenience, it seems your wife is contemplating divorce. I can see the headlines, the tearful little woman left abandoned by the husband she has stood loyally by all these years since she discovered that he was homosexual. Now found out for the rogue that he is, condemned and sent to Leavenworth for years. She can divorce him and swear off men for the future having established her credentials. How does that sound?"

"Wrong. In the first place, I am not homosexual. I have no interest in men or women. Children annoy me. I have friends of both sexes, I thought my wife was one of them. It seems sadly that I am wrong."

"Okay, what next?" Abby broke into the conversation. "I think there is someone interested in what is going on here, so we will need to do something pretty soon."

"Right. What is in the brief cases?"

The recovering agent Roth, now stirring, said nothing, nor did Meadows. Abby said, "let's take them anyway. We can check them out away from here."

Donny looked at Meadows. "You come with us." Ignoring Meadow's protests, Donny and Abby left the aircraft with Meadows still protesting. They left Roth in the aircraft still tied to his seat.

The mechanic, showing an interest, looked at his watch, got on a motorcycle and rode off. Donny and Abby bundled Meadows in the car and, with Abby driving, they left the airfield. They were going under the railway bridge when the explosion occurred. On the car radio there was a report of an explosion in the vicinity of the Aero club.

Donny said, "The mechanic on the motorbike, the man you thought was watching."

"Right. He looked at his watch and buggered off in a hurry." Abby recalled.

Donny thought for a moment. "Ring the police and say you saw a man in mechanics' overalls leaving the airfield in a hurry just before the explosion. I'll pass under a bridge and you'll lose the call. No names!"

Abby made the call and cut off at the crucial time. Donny stopped at a news stand and bought the most lurid paper there. "There is a number to call for news. Give them the same message."

With a grin Abby called, told the excited reporter the same story, then rang off.

Donny said, "They may not believe it but there may be someone saw the man roaring off. It could keep them off our trail for a while."

Meadows still looking bemused asked, "What is that all about?"

Donny looked at him pityingly. "You haven't worked it out yet, have you?"

Meadows shook his head "Worked what out?"

"My guess? The aircraft you were supposed to fly off in was supposed to blow up in the air. We kept it around on the ground so it blew up there. That is what caused the explosion we heard as we left. The frame was going to be fixed around you in absentia. After all dead men don't tell tales do they."

Abby rang the Accor hotel and booked a room using the false credit card. They made their way there. She checked in on her own, explaining that her husband would be along later with the luggage.

They smuggled Meadows into the room where they searched the two briefcases. Both contained a quantity of heroin and little else. The keys Meadows held would not open either case."

Donny and Abby looked at each other. Abby turned to Meadows. "Where were you due to land?"

"Washington International, we had nothing to hide on the way back."

She held up a pack, maybe a half kilo of powder. "Do you know what this is?"

Meadows, whose colour had returned, suddenly lost it all again. "Drugs," he said faintly, "Heroin?"

"This," she said, holding the bag up, "is what we in the business call 'the fall back.' If the main plot fails, there is always the transportation of drugs to fall back on. Once you're inside on drugs charges, all the other bad news can come out. Nobody will believe someone who uses his position to smuggle drugs."

Meadows slumped in his chair looking defeated. "What have I done to deserve this?" He wailed, looking desperate.

Donny took pity on him. "They have failed twice to get rid of you. My guess is they will try to kill you if they can find you. So we will see what we can do to keep you alive."

Abby was searching the cases for any clues. She found the little button locator. "Donny! Locator transmitters!"

He leapt to his feet. At the door he listened carefully, then opened it. "Bring everything." he said, going the wrong way down the hall and into the service elevator. In the basement he poured the heroin into the disgusting mess of spoiled food in the bins. He used an abandoned piece of stick to stir the powder in. They left the basement via the service entrance. On the street Abby went round to the car park and took the BMW. She had not given the number to reservations so it was not on record. By the time she got to the two men, both of the location buttons had been tossed into a truck destined for Stuttgart.

***

At the Campanile they booked Meadows in. He had his passport and cards, cash and the clothes he stood up in. They had visited a market on the way to the hotel. There they bought a soft bag and sufficient clothes for Meadows to change into and survive with for three days.

In the room Abby went to town. She made him dress in the casual sweatshirt and chino's they had bought. The trainers replaced the Oxfords Meadows had been wearing. His neat hair was dishevelled and trimmed by Abby, the uptight tight-ass was transformed into a slightly uncomfortable-looking, general-public lookalike. He was pushed over to the mirror. "Meet Don Meadows." She said.

Chapter Nine... Waiting for the other boot to fall

Gordon Meadows was stunned. He was not the person he had known all his life. He was a cool-looking dude, casual, laid back. The man he had known was uptight, fussy, dark suits and quiet tie, Crombie coat and brief case. This guy did not fit the picture at all. He found his shoulders relaxing from their normal tension. In fact he visibly loosened up as he saw himself reflected in the mirror.

What an odd feeling, he thought. *I cannot believe the difference it makes, not only to my appearance. I feel different!*

He turned around to Abby. "Thank you," he said simply. You have shown me a different person. Someone I did not know existed."

Abby was blunt. "It should keep you alive for a little longer anyway."

Donny said, "What exactly did happen when you visited the Holiday Inn?"

Without hesitation Meadows started talking. "I was met by a pretty girl at the door of their suite, Natalie Speight, I discovered. She was friendly but, obviously, I was not interested. The leader of the group was the man they called Remington, Paul Remington. He was Agent in Charge of the EU division CIA. There was another man there called Aaron Albrecht, American accent but definitely European nationality. I guessed he was muscle. He was one of those people who look friendly, but is as cold as ice inside.

"They unpacked the gun while I was there and checked it out. They spoke about the target, but at no time did they mention who it was. Remington mentioned the client on several occasions, also without naming names.

"I presume they were not too worried about me knowing what was going on. As a CIA employee, I was aware of some of the questionable things that they have done. Though I think it was more the fact that they had set up the kill protocol.

"The only thing I might be able to help with is, I think I know the location of the shooter in this business. Before I say more I know there is a chance that they are setting us up. But I received the information before anyone was aware of the Agency's part in this plan."

"What have you got to tell us about the location of the shooter?"

"The place they did not mention, but the situation I think they will use is not at the Parliament itself. It will be at the reception to be held in the residence of Count Bartelsky. He is, as you may know, one of the many movers and shakers in the European scene. His house is Chateau Tarquin, in its own grounds, parkland with trees."

"You seem well informed for a stranger to the country?" Abby said suspiciously.

"There was a program on the public service TV in Washington. It gave a description and tour of the grounds of the house. It has a history from the time of German occupation in the 18th Century. I read that the Count had purchased it, and I was aware that it was on the schedule for the visiting Heads of State. All will be in attendance. There are not too many places overlooking the area in front of the house where targets would be most vulnerable.

"If you google the map of the area you can probably work out what places are most suitable for the shooting to take place. The reason I thought of this place is that, if there is a problem shooting the German Premier, there will be alternative options available."

Abby looked up sharply at this comment, realising, that on the face of things, others of the group would also be suitable targets for the shooter. There was no particular reason why the French, British or Dutch heads should not create a similar stir in the political soup and allow advantage to go in another direction. For Russia it would take pressure off the efforts of Germany to stop Russian interference in the Balkans. If the British head fell, then it would delay the movement toward the re-establishment of British Sovereignty, leaving at best a commercial bond only with the EU. If the French head fell then the EU would probably fall apart, since the German-French alliance was the main thing keeping Europe together.

"Let's take a look and see for ourselves." Donny suggested. He turned to Meadows, "I know you look different and the better for it, but on this occasion I suggest you leave it to us, until you become a little better acquainted with the new you."

Meadows nodded, secretly happy to be left alone to get over the fact that his wife had been part of a plot to kill him, and the new person he had apparently become.

Tom and Lotte meanwhile had been wandering the area looking for lines of communication and watching the hotel as well. Tom was doing the hotel watch when all three recognised targets came out together. They were collected by a Ford Galaxy with dark windows. Aaron Albrecht was carrying the long gun box.

Tom called Lottie and Donny as he climbed onto his transport, a 150cc motorbike. Lotte responded, as did Donny. Donny told them of Chateau Tarquin, his current destination. "Tom, follow them direct. Lotte, catch up and support Tom. We are almost there already, if they are coming here

We'll meet up. If not, keep us in touch, Okay?"

Both Tom and Lotte acknowledged. Tom was already on the move, three cars behind the Galaxy.

They all met up in the public parking area near the main gates of the Chateau. The parkland and parts of the Chateau were open to the public. The quarters of the Count were in one wing of the building. The rent he paid contributing in no small way to the upkeep of what was considered by the people of France a serious piece of their history.

The two girls, arm-in-arm, wandered into the ticket kiosk and got tickets for all four of them. The building stood half a kilometre from the gates. The Galaxy had driven through and parked in the inner car park. There was no sign of movement from the silent vehicle. The black windows gave nothing away. It's presence was somehow menacing despite the sunny day and the people appeared to avoid it. Abby said, "Probably primal instinct," when Lotte commented on it.

Donny drove the BMW in and parked. He wandered across to look at some of the magnificent oak trees growing in the grounds. He was also giving the tree maintenance equipment the once-over. Particularly the cherry-picker, currently half extended as a man worked on the middle branches of the tree next to the one he was studying. He asked the worker about the trees. "Are you part of the staff here?"

"Yes. These trees are my babies." The man was good-humoured and chatted as he worked. Donny got round to the equipment. "Ha, that's better." The tree surgeon grinned, and answered. "All this equipment belongs to the estate. We are working all the woodland on this side at present, so we will lock up and leave the gear here until we finish at the week-end. Then we will move it all to the other side of the park next week perhaps, providing there is no emergency, perhaps a bad storm in the meantime." He shrugged in a typically Gallic fashion. "One never knows. The weather man says one thing. God says another?"

Donny left him and wandered off through the grounds, certain now how the shooter would set up. Using the cherry picker he would get a steady base for the shot at anyone near the main entrance to the Chateau. At 500 metres with the telescopic sights, he or she could not go wrong. If needed, a push at the right time to the platform, and the scapegoat was there. Likely to survive the fall? Probably a broken leg at least, and, with the rifle still on the platform, or better still on the ground nearby, who would believe him, or possibly her?

Thinking and wandering, he nearly missed the movement in the trees off to his right.

Without altering his pace, he called the others, "Anyone near the trees on the right of the road in?"

All three said 'no'.

Abby said, "In trouble again? I suppose I should come and get you out as usual?"

"I would rather you didn't. I will deal with this one myself. Just watch the road for reinforcements."

He clicked off the line and drew his automatic, still leaning against the tree trunk. He could hear the brush of feet through the grass on the other side of the tree. A foot hit the root on the other side of the tree. Donny watched as the man stumbled, cursing softly, into view.

Aaron Albrecht was not a happy man. He was a long way from his home in Hebron, close to the Dead Sea. The weather here in France was nothing like that shown in the holiday brochures. It was wet and cold and he missed the sun. The sight of Donny, standing looking over the barrel of a gun, did nothing to improve his mood.

"What is this for?" he said aggressively, pointing at the gun.

Donny was surprised, but impressed by the sang-froid of the Israeli. "It's just to ensure there is no, how shall I put it, misunderstanding while we talk.

"What have we got to talk about? I am just wandering in the grounds here enjoying the ambience of the place.

"I see. So there is no problem with the arrangements for the meeting at the weekend to be held here?"

"How would I know? I'm just a visitor. Who are you? Secret Police?" Albrecht sounded completely calm, confident, unruffled.

Donny was really impressed. "What about Remington? Is he happy with the arrangements so far?"

"How would I know? The only Remington I have ever heard of is the rifle that won the west."

Donny sighed. "Turn around and lean against the tree, feet out further. Lean on your hands."

As Albrecht leaned, still protesting, Donny removed the automatic from the waistband of his prisoner. "This will be the here for shooting rabbits, I presume?"

Albrecht shrugged. "A man should be prepared for anything, especially to defend himself in uncivilized surroundings."

"Like the heart of government in the EU, I presume?" Donny said, sardonically. "Ankle gun too perhaps?" He bent, carefully watchful for any attempt by Albrecht to lash out, as he checked both ankles and relieved the man of the small Colt 7.5mm automatic.

Rising, he said, "Do come and meet my friends. I know they will be happy to hear your opinions of the European Union and Hansie Krabbe, in particular."

The pair made their way to the main gate. Donny called Abby who brought the BMW. They carried Albrecht off to the river where they parked. Donny had a quiet word with Jonathon. "He has credentials showing he is a CIA agent, but I have the feeling he is actually Mossad or whatever they are called these days."

"What makes you think that?"

"He is too cool about this whole business. My feeling is that he is the replacement for Oskar as the scapegoat. Imagine, Israeli agent downs German chancellor. Not just the Muslim world, Europe, and the western world would all be down on Israel."

"I thought we were convinced that this was Russian inspired." Jonathon was doubtful.

"It still is. While the rest of the world is focused on the middle-east, Russia gains territory in its own backyard. The cries of the Eastern lands, lost in the turmoil of anti-Israeli feeling. By the time the situation is resolved the troops have moved in and peace restored. With the latest situation in Ukraine the disadvantages of the exclusive attention of the press can clearly be seen."

"Maybe you have a point. I suppose that Krabbe has no love for the Russians now she had the entire European Continent to play with. Boris Yeltsin started Russia down the slippery slope into the hands of the mafia. Now, with Shukov using the mafia to regain all the territories Russia lost, there is no love between the two countries any more. I'll send some assets to take your guest and keep him safe for the next few days. Where are you?"

Donny told him and went back to the car to brief Abby. The van from Jonathon arrived at 3.00 pm and took the impassive Mr Albrecht away. Donny steered the BMW back to the Chateau grounds. The motorbike was still there and they spotted Lotte coming from the trees where Albrecht had been captured. Lotte strolled over to the area near the BMW and started to talk. "Natalie and the big man went to look at the cherry-picker, then they looked around the area. They are back in the Galaxy at the moment. They were not happy."

"Did they spot you?"

"Nope. I am sure. As a ditzy blonde maybe. But as me, I do not think so."

Donny said, "A ditsy blonde? Are you kidding?"

Lotte looked at him sadly. "Poor old fellow, the years are not treating him well. Abby, you will need to educate the man better if we are to get along."

Abby laughed. "Sorry, Lotte. He is a bit slow today. Give him time. I'm sure he'll come around."

Donny ignored the comment and said, "The third member of the team is tucked away somewhere safe, so we can concentrate on the other two. Where are they, by the way?"

Lotte nodded her head to the other side of the car park. "Just over there. Why don't you two go back to the hotel and Tom and I will trail them back?"

"Right. We will get off now and see you back in the hotel." Donny smiled.

Abby called out, "Good luck." And they drove off.

***

Back at the hotel Abby went ahead to the room. Donny's attention was caught by the TV where a report on the explosion was being discussed. The reporter was asking the police officer, "Have you identified the two people killed in the explosion?"

"We believe, from scraps of clothing recovered that they were the aircraft crew, pilot and flight attendant, certainly a man and a woman. There was no sign of any other people involved."

"Was there any indication of the cause of the explosion?"

"The cause was a timed detonation of a block of some derivative of Semtex, probably intended to go off in flight. The aircraft we understand was, according to the flight plan lodged, delayed. It had been scheduled to depart 20 minutes before the explosion occurred. We are seeking help from the man who departed on a motorcycle just three minutes before the explosion occurred."

Donny went up to the room as the policeman gave the description of the motorcyclist passed on by Abby earlier.

In the room Abby was standing, glowing from the shower, clad only in a small towel, if clad qualified for the description.

"I was waiting for you to wash my back. You are too late now." Abby giggled.

Donny growled, "It's never too late, grabbed the towel and set off chasing Abby round the bedroom discarding clothes as he went.

***

Afterwards, as they lay side by side recovering from their shower, Donny mentioned the statement by the police officer. "It seems Michael Roth did not bother to release the aircrew. Which to me, means, he knew the bomb was there, and when it was due to go off. Indicating that he has been part of Remington's crew from the start."

"Probably had an excuse to leave the aircraft before it took off, and would not be able to rejoin it for some reason." Abby suggested.

"Sounds like they have a third member of their team once more. I sometimes think the great arranger in the skies has it in for us. One step forward two steps back, or at least mark time on the spot." Donny commented gloomily.

Abby laughed. "What a load of rubbish. You would be horrified if everything kept going right.

It's all the twists and turns the fickle finger of fate includes that keep you focused. Without the complications you would be bored stiff. Now, what's next?"

Donny turned toward her with a glint in his eye.

Abby rolled off the bed in a hurry. Oh, no. Let's not get carried away. We have work to do!" She grabbed her underclothes and started dressing.

Donny conceded with a sigh and dressed in turn. "Tomorrow, we must prepare. Friday, we must be on our toes. We need to save Natalie if possible. Remington is the target. And of course, save Frau Krabbe."

Abby said cattily, "I wondered if you were going to include her on the list?"

"What?"

"Hansie Krabbe is the entire reason we are doing this."

"Ah."

"What does that mean, Ah?"

"What I mean is that this entire operation was to establish Remington's true credentials and remove him from the chessboard."

"I believe we have achieved that end. We need to reinstate the status quo and ensure that Shukov gets a bloody nose."

Lotte called from the lobby. By the time she arrived at the room Donny and Abby were respectable once more.

The trio discussed the latest developments over room-service food. They deliberately made no firm plans until they knew what the opposition were doing over the next 24 hours.

Lotte's cell rang. She answered, listened briefly. "Okay, Tom!" She said and rang off.

"Remington is on the move, alone! He is in the lobby bar, waiting to meet someone. The concierge has been asked to steer his visitor to him in the bar."

"We'll go." Donny said, pointing at Lotte. Abby, you and Tom outside taking pictures, send them to Jonathon for identification. Go!"

All three dashed out of the room Donny and Lotte to the lobby and bar, Abby down the service elevator and around to the front to film whoever was of interest in the vicinity. Tom met her outside and both began waving cameras and snapping pictures. Abby posed in approved model style. Now bare of midriff, blouse tied under her bosom, barelegged with flirty skirt flung all ways, establishing her credentials.

The car arrived, disgorged three men, and the driver continued and parked the car. The important one stopped to enjoy the show, as Abby showed a hint of lacy panties in the poses she was adopting. She flashed a smile at the arrival. Tom threw a hissy fit at the men, who took the hint and continued into the hotel. "Did you get them all?" Abby asked.

"Hang on." Tom lifted the camera and snapped a picture of Abby, with the driver looking over her shoulder. "Got it," Tom said, "That's the lot."

The driver passed and went into the hotel to join the others. Tom dialled in Jonathon's cell number and sent a copy of the set of pictures for identification.

Abby tidied her blouse and tucked it more respectably into her waistband. Taking Tom's arm, they entered the hotel and sat in the lounge. Tom showed her the pictures, with and without the visitors. He sent a set to Donny's cell phone, then blew up the pictures of Abby, eliminating the targets from view. There was only one shot where that would not work, the last one he took of the driver. His doctoring was complete when one of the targets came over with the waiter carrying drinks for them. "Please be my guests. I saw the enchanting lady being photographed and I am curious. Should I know you?" His accent was American, with a hint of a Russian lilt.

Tom said, "We are busy. This is business. Go away!"

Abby laughed." Take no notice. Please, sit if you wish and thanks for the drinks. To answer your question, I think not-yet anyway. These shots are for my portfolio. Arturo," she indicated Tom, "said we needed to get commercial background shots. The hotel provided the sort of view he wanted. What Arturo wants, Arturo gets!"

The raised eyebrow of their companion said it all?

Abby understood and smiled. "In business matters only, Arturo is an artist with tastes of his own."

"You wish to see?" Arturo (Tom) fiddled with the camera and turned the 10cm by 6cm screen to show the interested man what they had been shooting. Approving comments followed the showing as, one after the other, Tom gave the man a preview of Abby's new portfolio. At the last picture with the driver's head looking over Abby's shoulder, Tom went, "Tsk. I will remove that one. The picture is good but I would need to photo shop that idiot out of the shot. I do not like this in a portfolio picture." He made to delete the picture. The man stopped him. "It is my friend, Nicolai. I am sure he would be very happy to have this picture. Is it possible, please? I will pay for it."

Arturo looked at him quizzically. Then he shrugged. "You have a cell phone, a smartphone?"

The man produced his iPhone.

Arturo said, "Is good. What is the number, please?"

The man gave his number. Arturo pressed buttons on the camera feature and the picture scrolled down on the iPhone screen. "So there it is. No charge. Now we go and produce the portfolio for my model."

He stood and took Abby's hand. "Come, Elise. We have work to do." He nodded to the Russian. "Enchante. A tout a l'heure, M'sieu." And left the lobby through the front door, with Abby being towed along behind.

Outside Abby could hardly contain herself. Once around the corner she burst out laughing, to be joined by a pale-faced Tom. "Arturo?" He said breathlessly, "Has his own tastes?" He collapsed as they staggered together through the service entrance. Abby straightened. "I will be known in future as Elise!" This created more giggles and it was with difficulty they managed to negotiate the route through the area to the elevator and thus back to the security of the room.

In the lobby the Russian was sending the picture to his embassy to establish the identity of the model, Elise.

***

In the bar Remington was drinking with the FSB agent delivering a message from Vladimir Shukov himself. "My leader wishes that the shooter takes the target agreed. On successful completion, it would suit him if the shooter tragically died. Complications can be avoided if the operation is terminated, finally. Is that understood?"

"Completely. Has the fee been transferred?"

"It has. Sent off this morning to the account you nominated."

"Good, I will check it now." Using his cell phone he dialled a number and watched the screen as the numbers scrolled through a sequence. Then an amount appeared that seemed to satisfy him and he closed the phone. I will complete my arrangements today. All will happen tomorrow as promised."

The Russian inclined his head and finished his drink. "Thank you, Mr Remington. I will watch the news with interest. Goodbye!"

He rose and left trailed by his escort.

The driver ran to fetch the car and drove to the hotel entrance. The Russians climbed in. As they drove off the cell phone of the Russian who obtained Tom's photograph of Abby rang. The message said Abby Marshall, M16. Then the car blew up.

In the hotel the explosion could be heard quite clearly. Remington smiled, rose from his seat at the bar, and returned to his suite.

Chapter ten...Actions speak....

Tom leaned out of the room window and looked at the cloud of smoke where the car had once been. "I suspect our fan has taken his last phone call. I presume Remington has been at work, or at least his mechanic."

Donny said, "It is obvious that the opposition is now up to four people, including the mechanic and Roth. Who will actually be the scapegoat? Could be any or all of the others. Remington is the only one that I'm sure will walk away from this."

Lotte laughed uncertainly. "You mean, that he would just allow all three to be either killed or arrested, as long as he walks free?"

Abby said, "I can confirm that for sure. His job, as Agent in Charge for the CIA, does mean that he has done this sort of thing many times already."

Tom looked around the room, Donny and Abby, a team in complete accord as far as he could tell. Finally Lotte. His eyes softened. Since their unconventional coming together he had become aware that being without her was not an option.

Without thinking, he walked over to her and gave her a hug. She looked up at him puzzled. "What?"

He kissed the tip of her nose. "Just because I felt like it." He smiled and she grabbed his head, pulled him down and kissed him properly. "Do it properly next time." She grinned and let him go.

From the other side of the room Abby giggled and said, "Would you like us to leave while you have a little time together?"

Lotte laughed and said, "Just because the romance has run out for you two old folks, you should not mock us youngsters."

Considering that Tom was older than all of them, and Lotte was only just younger than the others, that was pushing it. The general laughter following the comment eased the tension for them all.

"Tomorrow is the day if we have it right. Why don't we just lift them now and save ourselves the trouble tomorrow."

"Two things unfortunately against that. One being we may be wrong, and we are talking about a very senior officer in a sister service. The other is that the people involved in this matter cannot be taken without actual evidence. They have to be caught in the act." Donny explained.

Abby said, "As things stand, we know what is happening and where it is due to happen. All we have to do is be in the right place at the right time."

"They know of us. Roth knows you two, so you have to change your image in public." Tom was serious for the moment. "I would suggest that, in the circumstances, you two concentrate on the actual ambush at the cherry picker wherever they elect to raise it, if in fact they do. If Lotte and I try to keep in touch with the bodies themselves, we can keep you up to date with the actual shooting party."

"That works for me," Donny said. "If the plan goes as we predict, then I think we will have to watch our backs from all directions."

He got very serious looking, glancing at Abby. Abby exchanged looks and nodded. "I hate to bring the matter up but has it occurred to you that despite the importance of the task we are tackling, nobody apart from Jonathon has shown the slightest interest. This is despite the possibility that a very important person is about to be publicly assassinated. In addition the entire event is due to happen at the centre of Euro politics, arranged by a senior member of a US security agency.

"From what we have observed so far the threat is serious. People have already been killed. I think that confirms it is real. The team allocated to prevent this event is, in international standings, lightweight to say the least. Two professionals and two amateurs, I don't see others. This leads me to believe that we are possibly being used as a diversion for some other event that we know nothing of." He looked around the group. All were waiting. He had their exclusive attention. "From the events here so far, I think Remington has taken advantage of the situation, using the diversion to cover a genuine operation for his Russian employers. Now I considered putting this to our employers. Jonathon knows us well enough to accept the possibility. But he also knows our present boss would take a lot of convincing and we do not have the time. What it means is that we are on our own. I thought it would be best to clear the air, before we went hunting tomorrow."

***

In their own room that night Tom and Lotte truly discovered each other for the first time. The threat of possible serious injury or death became the critical point in their relationship. Though they had occupied the same bed for the past weeks, both had been willing to wait before taking the next step. The last barriers fell and they gave themselves fully without reservation, confident in their commitment.

***

For Donny and Abby there was a restless night, Donny feeling he was responsible for Tom and Lotte. He was aware that there were a whole bunch of matters he felt he should deal with.

One of the frustrations of command was that there was no one else to turn to when the questions came uphill. He mentioned the matter to Abby in the morning.

"Your trouble is you assumed the command stance without thinking ahead." Abby made the comment unsympathetically.

In truth there had been no chance to prepare. They had been involved in the matter without prior notice. "If you would be good enough to point out to me when I had the chance you refer to, I would be grateful. I have the impression that we have been trying to think on our feet since the entire affair started. There is also the fact that the events we are involved with have still not been explained to us by anyone including our beloved, supposed leader and confidante, Jonathon. We are where we are through serendipity, which means by lucky chance more or less."

Abby conceded the point, letting him off the hook. "We are all a bit frustrated being left out on a limb like this. It happens all the time for us, so we should be used to it by now."

After some thought in the matter, she commented, "We will just have to do what we usually do in the circumstances. Sort things out in our own way. After all 'needs must,' and it is what we are now paid for.

***

The BMW sighed to a stop. Its two occupants slipped out and melted into the shadow of the trees. The lights placed along the footpaths created broken shadows shifting and playing across the open places with the vagaries of the light breeze. The two figures, dressed in black and masked, were armed with holstered handguns. Each carried, in addition, a small hand-held crossbow that fired tranquilliser darts. They made their way through the trees to a point where they could observe the parked cherry-picker. They settled down and the minor disturbance of their progress ceased. The sounds of the woodland re-established and it was as if the intruders had never existed.

***

Paul Remington was exasperated. His contact at the Embassy had been uncooperative to say the least. The local agent had not been included in the need to know, and was not therefore willing to put himself out to help Remington with an extra team to cover the approaches to the woodland site.

"I have no orders apart from the instruction to cover the meeting with extra security. I have no one to spare for whatever operation you have ongoing. Perhaps if you could explain the nature of your operation I may be able to get extra help. What about it?"

Remington departed in disgust. The same old story was being peddled by the bean counters. People sitting in offices expecting too much for too little every time. Give them some bunch of guerrilla idiots in the jungle and they happily dispense millions. But ask to push the boat out for an in-house operation and there is always a reason why it cannot be done. Thoughtlessly expressing the opinion of servicemen the world over, and his current protagonists, he returned to the hotel to make the last minute arrangements with the three waiting there.

***

Natalie Speight picked up the Dragunov rifle with its cased telescopic sight. The heavy weapon with its smooth steel and polished wood was now familiar to her touch. There was a sensual feel to the weapon and she shivered as she contemplated the forthcoming task. Lining up the target in her mind, settling down in place, getting comfortable. Then, finger on trigger, waiting for the target to appear in view. Finally, the gentle squeeze of the trigger and the strike of the heavy bullet, the spurt of blood and brains, amid the shocked group of unknowing people in the area. Thinking about it gave her an almost sexual reaction. She carefully put the gun to one side.

Roth saw her with the gun and smirked at her reaction. "Feel like some bedtime boogie, Nat?"

"In your dreams, little man." She turned away from him in disgust.

He stepped over and grabbed her, spinning her round and grabbing her face. He bent and kissed her, her shocked face inflaming him. His hand dropped to her breast and he squeezed her, pushing her against the table. Reaching behind her, she grabbed the Glock laid on the table with the other weapons. Lifting it, she slammed it against the side of his head. Stunned, he fell back. She hit him again, spitting words at him. "How dare you! You cheap little second-rate hood. Keep you dirty hands to yourself. She lifted the gun to hit him again. Her hand was grabbed and the blow never landed.

Remington was standing, holding the gun she had used.

"I thing you made your point." Remington said. "Roth was out of line. He's paying for it now. The matter finishes here!"

Natalie shrugged and rubbed her breast where Roth had grabbed it. With her other hand she wiped her mouth. "Just keep the animal away from me, or I will kill him."

Remington grinned, "It will all be over tonight. You won't have to put up with him for long." He turned to the battered man. "Get out of my sight and get on with the job I gave you."

Roth left the room, holding his hand to his head. He looked murderous.

Remington returned his gaze to Natalie. "You okay?" He reached out and touched her breast where she had been grabbed. She did not flinch or try to evade his touch.

"I'm okay," she said. "He just lost it, I think."

"It's not good enough. He is supposed to be a professional. It will not happen again."

At that point Roth sealed his fate. His forged papers as an agent for CIA would be withdrawn and doctored to demonstrate the forgery. A new version of his history would be allowed to come out, proving his association with a radical German Nazi group.

His body would be found with the gun, beside the cherry-picker.

***

The assassination team, followed by Tom and Lotte, left the Holiday Inn at 7.00 pm. Tom called Donny and Abby updating them. Both had only just settled in position in at the woods. They anticipated the arrival within the next half hour.

When the party appeared their four-wheel drive hooked up to the cherry-picker and made off slowly through the trees.

Donny and Abby trotted after them, keeping up easily with the slow progress of the towing vehicle between the trees. The vehicle stopped and the trailer was unhooked. The power cable remained attached to the four-wheel drive. Natalie and the rifle got onto the platform. She operated the control and it began to rise. Donny and Abby arrived to see the platform begin to move. Remington got out of the car and called to Natalie. "Make yourself comfortable. You'll be there the best part of an hour."

"That's okay. I'm fine." She answered quietly, obviously perfectly calm.

Abby was chilled by her calmness in view of the impending shooting. "How can she envisage stay calm, when she intends killing someone in an hour's time."

Donny looked at her. "Come on, Abby. Some of the people we have been in contact with have been just as bad."

"I suppose so. It's just that there is every chance that she would have got away with it, had we not been here."

"You get up the tree opposite. Do not let her know you are there."

Abby left Donny and started up the side of the tree away from the ambushers.

An astonished Donny saw Remington, and the man he realised must have been the mechanic. get out of the car, carrying another man. They positioned him beside the base of the cherry-picker, sprawled as if he had fallen from above. The man was evidently dead. The mechanic went off through the trees and returned ten minutes later riding an off-road bike. He parked it and stood a helmet on the seat. "Natalie?" He called quietly, "The bike is here with your helmet. Take it easy in the woods."

"Thank you, Charles. Good luck!" Natalie's voice sounded quietly serene.

Abby, now ensconced in the tree beside the platform, smiled to herself. "You are mine, bitch. I'll wipe that smirk off your face."

***

The suppressed Glock was cocked and locked in her waistband. As she peered round the tree she could see the other girl lining up her rifle at the distant target.

She drew the Glock from its place and leaned round the trunk, holding the gun in her left hand. Slipping the safety-catch off she fired, just as Natalie started to squeeze the trigger on the Dragunov. The sound of the Glock was lost in the rustle of the leaves. The shot from the rifle echoed through the woodland, the sound shocking in comparative silence of the parkland.

The bullet punched a hole in the front wall of the Chateau, the impact un-noticed as the crowd outside turned to see the origin of the sound of the shot, which had been heard carried by the breeze. No other shots were heard. The heads of state attending were all swiftly ushered into the Chateau.

On the platform Natalie was looking at the rifle and the scar where Abby's bullet had struck the metal casing of the lock mechanism. The automatic reloading was jammed solid. "Shit!" She cursed the gun without really thinking about the fact that the gun had been hit by a bullet, causing her to miss her shot. She threw the gun to the ground below and started the platform for the ground. Abby jumped onto the platform grabbing, and half choking Natalie. She reacted, wrenching Abby's hands away from her throat and hitting her temple with her elbow. Abby collapsed, stunned to the floor of the platform. Natalie was able to get off, and run to the parked motor-bike. Donny started to his feet as Natalie kicked the bike into life and roared off, the helmet strung on her arm. Abby leaned shakily out of the platform.

"What happened?" Abby gasped.

"They all got away." Donny said dryly, "Except him," Nudging the body of Roth with his toe. As soon as Natalie was up in the air, the four-wheel drive took off. The platform lowers itself without the need of power. Remington and the mechanic were in the car together. Natalie got away on the bike."

"Why didn't you stop her?" Abby said.

"Because you were crawling out of the platform looking wounded. We'll catch them soon enough. Tom and Lotte are on their tail already."

As he spoke, the vibration of the cell phone warned him a call was coming in.

"Come on, let's get out of here before somebody comes and arrests us for uncommitted crimes."

He took her arm and made off through the woodland to the spot where they had parked the car. Putting the cell phone to his ear he said, "Yes!"

Tom and Lotte were on the road to Nancy. Speaking to Donny, he said, "Natalie has just passed us going like her ass is on fire. I get the impression that something went wrong."

Donny said, "She missed!"

Tom smiled. "Good, I know someone else who will be pleased." Donny heard Tom saying "She missed." Then he came back on the line.

"What's next, boss?"

"Keep on their tail and keep us posted. Do not get caught."

"That we will do." Tom smiled as he rang off. "More of the same," he said to Lotte.

He pushed the speed up a little keeping the tail light of Natalie's bike in view in the distance ahead. The tracker indicated that Remington was turning right off the main road.

"What sort of place is that?" Tom asked as they approached. Lotte studied the map which the others had insisted was old-fashioned and out of date. "Am

I being asked if the place is marked on my aged map?"

"Yup!" Tom grinned. "You certainly are. What exactly does that antiquated thing say about the building?"

"It says, smarty-pants, that people who refuse to recognise the utility of tried and true methods deserve the frustration of being told to find out for themselves."

Tom stopped the car and turned to the giggling girl seated next to him. One hand clamped on the seat-belt lock. The other grabbed her chin and turned her head to face him. He kissed her with verve and at the same time wrenched the map from her hands. She grabbed his ears with both hands and would not let him draw back from the kiss.

It was wasted effort. Tom made no attempt to draw back. Letting the map drop beside his seat, his hand unlocked her seat belt and dragged Lotte onto his lap. He proceeded to make the most of the occasion.

Eventually, they separated. The map was produced and perused. The map indicated that the building in question was a hotel/spa. Obviously once a mill, the sign on the road was Ruc dc Moulin.

Tom called and informed Donny where they were, and indicated that both Remington and Natalie had gone to the hotel. "We are going to check it out and take a room, if we can. Lotte is tired and it looks from here as if our friends are staying overnight, at least."

"Good. Abby and I will locate in the area, away from where you are. I would really like to clear this matter up as soon as possible. Just be careful. Both Natalie and Remington have shown that they are quite ruthless."

Donny rang off. He was worried. Abby looked at him, then dressed. She had been prepared to get to bed despite the comparatively early hour. She looked at the clock, 10:12 pm. "Let's go. They could need back-up and we are doing no good here."

Relieved, Donny grabbed his jacket and keys and they went out to the car. The BMW made short work of the national road to Obernal. On the A35 they turned off at junction 13 to St Pierre.

They identified the hotel, across the field. They parked off the road and made their way across the field to the hotel garden. There were people wandering around the area so Donny and Abby wandered arm-in-arm like the others they could see, chatting and strolling in the pleasant evening air.

Lotte and Tom were sitting with drinks by the pool. Abby wandered over, did the kiss-kiss with them both, then seated herself to talk with Lotte while Tom searched for a waiter for another drink.

Donny drifted through the hotel until he found Remington and Natalie sitting in the bar.

They were doing a good imitation of a pair of lovebirds, holding hands and kissing whenever their eyes met. The age difference was apparent, but in this day the sight was no longer unusual.

Either they were better actors than he gave them credit for or there was more than a little realism in their canoodling. Donny shrugged, Natalie, for all her attitude, was a very shapely, sexy-looking woman. Remington was what some might call a hunk, big trim and rugged looking.

Donny wondered where the other man was. He set off in search of him.

The man was leaving the deserted car park when Donny spotted him. There was a little nag of suspicion in the back of his mind. The man may have left something in the car. But maybe there was another reason. Donny scanned the car used by Tom and Lotte. He found a device slipped under the driver's seat, that depended on a small trembler switch. Inactive at present it was activated by a small electrical relay. Once triggered the first bounce or bump, or even the driver sitting heavily would set the device off. Donny slipped his driving licence between the poles of the trembler and removed the bomb. Looking around he spotted the Range Rover used by Remington. He went over to the vehicle, the doors were locked. He walked around the parked vehicle. In the shadow between this car and the next he dropped to the ground and looked underneath. Between the exhaust pipe and the chassis there was space for him to force the bomb between the two. Leaving the trembler facing him, he carefully removed the licence from between the points and slithered out from beneath the vehicle.

He guessed that the circuit would be made live in the morning after Tom's car had gone. He went to join the other three and got the key to lock Tom's car. He made sure the bomb had not reappeared before he locked the car.

With things adjusted as best he could, he settled for the status quo at the moment, but warned Tom to check carefully before opening their car just in case. For his own peace of mind Tom checked the car and put a tell-tale in place, just in case of a break-in he may not spot.

***

The following morning the motorcycle had gone and so had Remington and Natalie, The Range Rover had been taken by the other man, who was surprised when he switched the power on to his surprise package. The Range Rover went up with a satisfying bang, disintegrating and distributing itself and the driver over several square metres of landscape.

On the motorbike, Remington and Natalie heard the bang behind them. Both jumped to the same conclusion and smiled. For Tom the frustration of losing the tracker was alleviated by the noise of the bomb going off. As he and Lotte picked their way past the hole in the road and the shattered car, he reflected that playing with fire could mean getting burnt.

They found the motorbike abandoned at the aerodrome de Rene Fonck at Remomeix. A private jet had collected two people from the aerodrome, and the direct trail had gone.

Chapter Eleven...Don't shoot the messenger

For Donny and Abby, the result of sending in the report of the Remington affair was, as Donny described it, a 'right bollocking' from the Director. As she pointed out, their instructions clearly stated that Remington and what he did was none of their business. It appeared that their reported conflicts with the rogue CIA personnel had been put down to over-reaction and misunderstanding.

Jonathon gave them a pat on the back which meant more to them that the words of the Director.

Tom and Lotte were retained on a temporary basis, which as Jonathon pointed out, was the basis of their employment in the beginning.

The Director would not, as a result, countenance any action to have the actions of Paul Remington investigated or even discuss the removal or punishment of Paul Remington. She was, in the opinion of those who knew her, captivated by the big rugged traitor. Discreet enquiry revealed that Natalie was now living with Remington in his Georgetown house.

The team were once more back in the routine of completing the university stage of their lives. Prepared to start life in Chambers in London as trainee barristers, they were now searching for a suitable apartment in the London area. Tom and Lotte were also searching for the home they were going to set up. They had found a Victorian house in Ealing which they were having restored. Since Donny and Abby were looking, and the house was ideal for conversion into two apartments, they offered to share the cost. It enabled all four to move in sooner rather than later.

***

Paul Remington was ostensibly clear of all suspicion. Despite his relocation in the CIA Headquarters in Langley as Deputy Director, Europe, he was under no illusions that there were enemies in the directorate who were waiting for the slightest slip, now he was under the eye, as it were. Natalie had slotted into his life surprisingly well. Her nature was based on a more adult outlook that the average women of her age. She realised that, apart from accepting Paul as a reasonable bedmate, he had plans for the future that she wanted to be part of. It meant that she was required to live with him, but with the end in view, it could be worse.

Not a man given to unnecessary vindictiveness, Paul Remington was however determined to find out what had gone wrong with the operation in

Europe. He was unaware of the fact that Natalie already knew, but had not, up to now, told him.

It was an inadvertent slip on her part, which gave the game away. In conversation on another matter, the names Donny Weston and Abby Marshall came up, with their exploits in the Florida Keys being discussed. Nadine was intrigued at the mention of the pair. Then another of the guests said, "Surely they were involved in the European business where Paul Remington was involved."

On hearing this, Remington looked at Natalie as she confirmed that they were present.

Natalie was not surprised at the introduction of the subject when they returned to his Georgetown house. "I said nothing, because there was no point at the time. I knew they were involved as were Tom Hardy and Lotte Compton."

"Why didn't you mention them at the time?" He was looking angry, to her surprise.

She felt her own annoyance at this interrogation. "The team you were using in the field were pretty inept. They did not even realise who or what they were up against. In my mind I decided to let your so-called professionals handle things. They managed to demonstrate just how unprofessional they were. Wherever you dredged them up from, they were a waste of space and time."

The slap came out of the blue. Paul Remington was standing over her, trembling with anger and frustration.

Natalie felt her face. It was hot and stinging from the force of the slap.

As she rose to her feet she was aware of Paul standing his hand half raised, as if to strike her again. She straightened, standing fully upright looking up into Paul's eyes. Her hand moved fast. The impact on his cheek was loud and hard. He stood stunned, unbelieving.

"You ever lift a hand to me again and I will kill you." There was pure ice in Natalie's voice.

Paul Remington stood for a moment longer. Then he turned and, as he walked away, said, "Get out of my house, bitch. Take your crap with you."

She heard him slam the front door. Then the car started up. The tyres squealed as he left in a hurry.

Nadine did not have much of her own there, just clothing, toiletries and money. She swiftly gathered her things, called a cab, and left the Georgetown house that night. She left the USA the following morning, via Canada.

***

Tom Hardy received a cryptic text message. It referred to nemesis in a second encounter for the quartet. *'PR et al, is on the prowl, after blood. Love, Natalie'.*

The signature was to upset Lotte. Natalie admitted to herself that she quite fancied Tom, but pragmatically dismissed any ideas in that direction. But she had no compunction at spoiling things for Lotte if she could.

On receiving the text, Tom contacted Donny. There seemed little they could do about matters until something happened, apart from being prepared to react if anything came up.

Donny's reaction was to inform Abby and let Jonathon know. He did also ensure they was armed at all times, if only with the Kevlar knives which passed barriers without registering.

***

Paul Remington's anger was deep-seated, based on an imagined insult from an insensitive M16 agent after the Florida incident Natalie had mentioned. Remington had been agent in charge of the Florida gateway, a sub-rosa conduit in and out of the country, used by the CIA to avoid embarrassment. He had been unaware of the part his superiors and colleagues played in the importation of drugs, mainly cocaine. The dismantling of the network which transpired through the intervention of the two British agents, Weston and Marshall, had spelled an end to his field activities.

He had hated the office. He would never get anywhere through his office skills, basically because he had none. When his equally-driven Director had dreamed up the assassination scenario to destabilise the EU set-up and placed him back in the field in charge, his desire to be out there overcame any scruple he may have had for performing such a lunatic scheme.

With the dismissal of his Director, to live out his life in an institution, the part played by Remington was judged to be astute handling of an impossible situation by a loyal but sensible employee, and rewarded as such. His current appointment was recognition that he had not only handled the problem, but had swept it away without collateral damage to the agency.

Remington understood he had got out of a difficult situation smelling of violets. Promotion for failure was not that common. His gratitude however did not extend to the true reason the scheme had failed. His own opinion of the planning and execution of the operation was that the perfect plan had been spoiled by the blundering interference of the four British agents, whose luck had been exacerbated by the ineptitude of the mercenaries he had been forced to employ.

He was already regretting his reaction to Natalie's awareness of the part played by the British four. Her input, he realised now, had been helpful in the moments when quick decisions had to be made. He shrugged. She had been fun in bed, too. Seated in his now empty house, he contemplated his options.

As Deputy Director he could travel to Europe at will. The use of the Gulfstream or the Citation was only subject to the demands of his superiors who were becoming fewer as he rose through the ranks.

His researches had shown that Weston and Marshall were both now serving in the Inns of Court in London as trainee barristers, (Attorneys,) learning their way in through the British High Court system. It would not be an impossible task to snatch them, take them to some quiet spot and interview them. The girl, Abby, would be fun to play with and whoever he used could have her to finish off, after he was done with her. Her partner could watch. That would make the revenge, just a little sweeter.

He must not forget the other two, Hardy and Compton. Lotte, another interesting prospect, a pretty thing he recalled, and the man, Tom Hardy. There was an agent they called Silk. She was perfect for the operation to deal with a man like Tom. She specialised in acupuncture, with pain!

There was time. Let them relax. Tom and Lotte in the Mediterranean and Donny Weston and Abby Marshall in London. He would strike when ready, not before.

Paul Remington went to his lonely bed, warmed by the thought that his revenge would come cold and tasty, at his pleasure.

***

Tom Hardy had earned himself a reputation in a small circle of sailing people, and while in Valetta, he and Lotte had managed to perform several yacht deliveries throughout the Med.

Lotte's grandparents were now committed to living out their lives on the Sp*eedwell.* Neither really wanted to stay in the bungalow they owned at Montrose. Tom and Lotte were offered the bungalow as a home to do with as they wished. As Mary pointed out they had left it to her in their will anyway, so they were quite happy to gift it to her now, "Call it a wedding present," Will said with a smile. "After all, we won't live forever. Though we're liable to survive a bit longer here than we would in the gales of the North Sea."

So, after three months getting tanned in the Mediterranean and collecting a useful addition for the bank account for their delivery efforts, Tom and Lotte flew to Edinburgh, hired a car and drove north to Montrose, and the bungalow gifted to them by Will and Mary.

***

Natalie Speight was contemplating her future. Her father, recovered now from his injuries was keeping a low profile, disassociating himself from the 'friends' he had been involved with when he encountered the *Speedwell* in the English Channel. He was happy to have her at home once more. In his own words, "Never did trust the big American bastard."

She smiled cynically. Natalie had no illusions about her father. But he was still her father. She was sitting in the coffee-shop window when she saw Lotte and Tom wandering along Montrose High Street. She hesitated for a moment, then knocked on the window to get their attention. Startled, Lotte looked up and saw her.

Natalie beckoned them in, lifting her coffee cup to reinforce the invitation.

Lotte looked at Tom. He shrugged, so they came in.

Natalie ordered another pot of coffee. "I realise you two do not have anything in common with my dad and me, but..." She hesitated then waited while the coffee was poured out for the others. "As you may know I was involved with Paul Remington. I am no longer. He has discovered the working relationship between you two, and Donny Weston and Abby Marshall. Have I got that right?"

Tom nodded, saying nothing, waiting to see what she had to say.

Natalie continued. "Between the four of you, you managed to bugger-up some operation that his insane boss had cooked up to destabilise Europe, would you believe? The result being his boss lost his job, and is now in some nut house in Alabama. Remington got his job."

She paused to drink coffee and collect her thoughts. Then continued, "Paul has become aware that the reason everything went belly-up in Europe was that you four, basically found out what was going on, and put a spanner in the works. He had not realised that you four had been the cause of his problems there. He is a micro-planner who is not as good as he thinks he is. He also has the delusion that he is a natural field operative. I stress delusion. I think he is below average in reality, and, as you must have realised, can be blindsided fairly easily by a decent pro."

At this point Lotte broke in. "This is interesting, I confess. But what has this to do with us?"

"I was just coming to that. Paul is now Deputy Director in the CIA. His idiot bosses think that he, with tact and discretion, got them out of an embarrassing situation and promoted him to take control of the European Scene. They were not aware that his idiot boss had followed Paul's suggestion for the assassination job. Now that Paul is aware that he was frustrated by you four he is out for payback, big time."

Tom laughed. "Wow, and just how does he propose to arrange that?"

"To start with, the boss of M16 has a thing for him. She apparently was asked to intervene with his bosses over the European Operation. But the stupid woman would not be told, and refused. I would guess that Remington will start by pressuring her to suspend or dispense with the services of all four of you. Then he could issue a contract without involving M16 and dispose of you all."

Lotte looked at her, stunned for a moment. Then she turned to Tom.

He looked thoughtful. "That would work. I think we should contact the others, sooner rather than later!" He looked at Natalie, "You have no reason to like us. Why?"

Natalie sat back and thought for a few moments before she answered. "When Paul discovered he had been outfoxed, he also found out that I knew. He hit me, because I had not told him, and I had not warned him about you four. How or why I was supposed to know that Donny and Abby were pros, or that you two were naturals, I do not know. I do know that he is a fool and he could get away with this one. He is dangerous and needs to be stopped. And the bastard hit me." She sat back as Tom nodded slowly, understanding the hurt underlying that final simple statement.

They left Natalie and made their way back to the bungalow. Lotte rang Abby and passed on the news. "I'll get back to you as soon as I know something." Abby said.

Lotte put the phone down, turned to Tom and said, "We wait!"

Tom went through to the bedroom and returned with their two Walther PPK's. Passing hers to Lotte he said, "From now on we carry, everywhere."

Chapter Twelve...Sticks and Stones.

Donny looked serious when Abby told him what Lotte had said. "What had Jonathon got to say?"

Abby looked at him quizzically. "You've forgotten. He called last week. He is undercover in Georgia at the moment, having a stab at the Russians. He will be out of contact for at least another couple of weeks."

"Ah, yes. I should have remembered. Well, knowing how popular we are with our leader, we should be prepared to look after ourselves. From now on we stay tooled-up. Make sure you carry your Number 10 'permit to carry'. I do not trust our lady boss." Donny referred to the special firearms permits issued to them by the PM himself, following a series of close encounters on both sides of the Atlantic. The control of M16, becoming more and more a political football, meant that agents, who become targeted for whatever reason, could be deprived of their personal protection at the whim of the appointee. After consideration the Prime Minister some years ago considered the matter and decided the risks were justified.

Overriding the gun-permits issued by the Commissioners of Police and the Directors of Security M15, M16, the PM's permit prevailed.

They carried arms from then on.

The first sign of trouble came with a message from the Director to the Head of Chambers where the pair were under pupillage. Standing before Sir Edward Trevallian, feeling very much the naughty school kids, they were gratified to hear that the Director of M16 had been in touch.

"How well do you know Dame Mary Fitch?"

Donny answered for both. "We know her, Sir, but not well."

"She appears to know you two. To the extent that she is demanding that I dismiss both of you from my chambers under threat of repercussions. Have you anything to say?"

Donny looked stunned. "Does she give a reason?"

"Apparently not. Security, it seems. Now, Donald, I have known your father and uncle since we were at University together. Have you done anything to merit your dismissal?"

"Absolutely not, sir. Neither Abby nor myself has committed any offence against the nation, nor anyone else to our knowledge."

Sir Edward sat back in his chair. "One more thing. The Fitch woman says she has withdrawn your permits to carry arms. Are you carrying arms?"

"We are both armed, sir. If we may, we will show you the permits we have. They are not within the competence of the Director to revoke." He and Abby produced their permits.

Sir Edward asked, "Why?"

"We are both members of the security service. When Madam Fitch took over she was immediately against our presence. She has attempted to have us removed ever since."

"And the permits?" Sir Edward tapped them against his desk.

"The PM believed that, with our record of success, we would be at risk from many different sources. We are therefore permitted to carry arms for self-defence, at all times. Though, I hasten to add, we do not always carry arms."

"Why now?"

"We are aware that the CIA have discovered that we prevented a plot by a renegade agent to de-stabilise the EU. The Europe Director for the CIA is a friend of Madam Fitch. We were warned that the CIA is not happy with our interference. We believe pressure has been brought to make us vulnerable to attack. Revenge, I suppose. Using hired help to keep their hands clean."

The astonished look on Sir Edward's face said it all.

Donny said, "I know it sounds like a bunch of kids playing rather lethal games. But I assure you it is true."

Abby broke in. "Sir, there are very nasty people out there. Life is cheap to the big organisations involved in espionage. The operation we interrupted was the attempted assassination of the German Chancellor at the recent European summit."

Donny looked at her, shocked at her revelation of the last operation they had been involved in.

Sir Edward said, "How did you know about that?"

Donny answered.. "We stopped them. The shot went wild."

"Where was that?" Sir Edward asked quietly.

"Strasbourg," Donny said. "On the patio in front of the venue. The shot was taken from a cherry-picker nearly one half mile away."

Sir Edward handed the licences back. "I believe you. I do not want to know more. Take whatever time you need to clear this matter up. I will clear matters with the clerk. Good luck."

Donny and Abby left the Chambers carrying their brief cases, but leaving their robes and wigs in the lockers.

"I wonder how Sir Teddy knew about the attempt on the Chancellor?" Donny said.

Abby was quiet for a few moments not answering Donny's question. "On the other side of the road. Two men with a weapon. In the van parked in the delivery lay-by." She said.

Donny did not hesitate. He grabbed her hand and spun round, reversing their direction totally. The open door of the office building beside them was the immediate choice. They entered on the run. The small shower of stone from the silent impact of the bullet indicated how close the shooter had come.

They ran through the building and exited through the side door. They split up. Donny crossed the side road and walked quickly to the main road where the van had been parked. Not surprisingly, it was no longer there.

Abby on the other side of the road crossed and went to the spot where the van had been standing. Donny saw her stoop and pick up something. He followed her to the bus stop opposite Lincoln's Inn Fields.

As the bus arrived they allowed the few people waiting to board, and started to board themselves. Instinct made Donny look up at the passenger seating herself opposite the bus door. She lifted her head and her eyes met his eyes for a moment. Donny stepped off the platform pulling Abby with him, saying for the benefit of any onlookers, "Oops! Wrong bus. we need the other stance."

The bus pulled away before the woman Donny noticed could react.

"What was that all about?" Abby asked.

"Instinct!" Donny said, "Let's take a walk."

They wandered down Drury Lane, ending up in the Strand.

At the Savoy they wandered in. Donny checked them in to a double room. He nodded to the concierge as he passed him. The man watched the door checking the other people entering, without making it obvious.

As soon as they reached their room, the door closing behind them was prevented from shutting by a shiny black polished shoe.

"Mr Weston, how nice to see you again. I am afraid this room has already been reserved for others. If you would come with me, I will take you to another room." Leading the way the concierge escorted them to a room on the next floor. He presented them with two key cards and a holder identifying them as Mr and Mrs Andrews.

As he sat down on the bed, Donny sighed. "I forgot that we had been introduced by Jonathon when we were here last. I realised I knew Antoine, the concierge, when we came in. But I had forgotten the system they followed with our people. Seeing Antoine at the door gave me a shock, until I recalled how it worked. Let's hope Madam Fitch is not aware of it. By now any record of our being here will be gone."

In fact at the reception desk the lady enquiring for Mr Weston or Miss Marshall was being politely told there was no person of that name registered in the hotel. She was asked to leave her details. If and when a Miss Marshall or Mr Weston registered she would be informed.

Oddly, she declined the offer and left the Savoy frustrated at losing the trail of the pair.

In their room Donny used his codex cell phone to call Tom Hardy. He got through and, recognising Tom's voice, he said, "Tom, where are you? Is Lotte with you?"

"In reverse order, yes, and Watford Gap Services on our way to the Ealing apartment."

"If you are not being followed already, watch out for a trail car. Check your own car with the bug detector, just in case you have a tracker attached. If you find one put it on another car going your way, south toward London."

"What's happening at your end?" Tom asked.

"We have been put on someone's contract. Already one missed shot on the street, would you believe. Also it seems our revered director had cast us adrift, cancelled our permits etc."

"But she can't."

"I know, but she doesn't, thank goodness. We are at the Savoy laying low at the moment. Join us here and we'll work something out between us." He passed on the current room number and suggested they were discreet about it.

***

Later, with Tom and Lotte in their room, the four discussed the latest developments. As Donny put it, "Things were going haywire because they had between them saved what could have been a world conflict at worst, and an acute embarrassment, at best for the most powerful nation in the world, so called."

"What we are up against is what my lecturer would call ego. Remington's obsession with being 'James Bond', and Madam Fitch with being 'M'." Abby's comment had a bite they were unaccustomed to hearing from her normally cheerful voice.

Tom shook his head. "Up to now I thought we were all playing games. But the shooting so far has convinced me that this is serious. Natalie was not kidding with her comments on Remington. The man is psychotic. Unfortunately, with the fact that our so-called leader prefers his truth to ours, we are left with a situation where we must put up or shut up, and neither prospect is good."

Lotte interjected, "Surely we can speak to a control officer in M16 and get something working for us. They must, like Jonathon, be aware that the woman is a romantic idiot!"

Abby said thoughtfully, "It's not that simple. What might work is if we could get Natalie and Fitch together. Perhaps Natalie could convince her that Remington is nuts and highly dangerous to both

USA and UK. It seems obvious that he has his bosses fooled." Abby sat back and added. "Otherwise we need to disappear until Jonathon returns at least. That could be days, weeks, even months. For Donny and me, that would be the end of our law career, as barristers anyway."

The four friends sat considering their options. None seemed to feel optimistic about their prospects.

***

The knock on the door was quiet. Donny held up his hand and stopped the murmur of conversation. The knock was repeated. He got to his feet, gun in hand and being cocked without conscious thought. He moved to the door. Abby already on her feet gun in hand, moved to the other side of the door.

Tom and Lotte, not quite as fast, took position behind the settee, guns drawn and ready.

Donny looked round and nodded in approval. "Who is it?" He asked.

"Antione, M'sieu."

Donny snatched the door open and Antoine stepped in.

He spoke quickly and clearly, "Sir, there are men seeking you. Other staff have seen you in the hotel. They will not realise who you are. Please, for your own safety, you must leave here now."

Donny indicated Tom and Lotte, "My colleagues as well?"

"All of you! They have your pictures., I said I
had seen you come in and I thought, leave later.
Others have said otherwise. If they press, they have
warrant cards. This room would be searched and
future use would be compromised. So, I will lead
you out. You will be seen on the street. Is there a
place you can go?"

"Yes there is. Lead on, Antoine. And thanks for
the heads-up." Abby collected her bag and coat. She
removed a grey-haired wig from the bag, and
slipped it on. Glasses with black rims followed,
with straight back, coat slung over her shoulders,
she became an elderly habitué of the hotel.

Antoine stepped out into the corridor and collected a wheelchair, with rugs and a coat. He indicated Tom to sit. With one rug over his knees and
the other round his shoulders, he sat unsure what to
do next. Lotte ran through to the bathroom and returned with talcum powder. Donny wheeled Tom
through and Lotte tipped a liberal amount onto
Tom's hair, and with a sweep of her hand, transformed his neatly-combed hair into wild disarray of
grizzled, mainly dirty white hair. "Now stoop!" She
said. Tom's shoulders dropped under the rug. "Better." Lotte said. She donned a fair short wig, and her
coat, then pushed Tom into the corridor. Donny accepted a coat from Antoine, (the doorkeeper was

roughly the same build) and took Abby's arm. They followed the chair with Lotte pushing, along to the service elevator. The rather spartan, but roomy cabin took the entire party. The concierge pushed the button for the garage, and the elevator descended at a stately pace.

***

The watcher saw nothing unusual in the party being assisted into the limo which arrived to collect them. He did not notice that, when the limo left, the concierge was putting the wheelchair into the store room, along with the rugs and in fact the spare coat, which also escaped notice.

The concierge, seeing the watcher apparently for the first time said, "What are you doing here?"

The man produced a warrant card, "Keeping an eye out for someone," he said brusquely.

Antoine shrugged and with a wry smile returned to his duties in the hotel foyer.

Chapter thirteen...Hide and Seek

The limo driven by Antoine's son-in-law swept down the Strand. "Where to, boss?" The driver asked in pure cockney. Seeing Donny's indecision in his mirror, the driver said, "I'm Antoine's son-in-law. He said you're good. So whatever you say goes, and no questions." He tapped the side of his nose.

"Out of the way somewhere, if you don't mind. We would like to drop out of sight for a while."

"Gotcha, my name's Charlie, by the way. Charlie Manners. My place is in Wapping, down river. I'll take you to the 'Isle of Dogs'. My mate has a boat to hire there on the river. It's a bit of alright for four. He had a bit of bother so I'm looking out for his interest while he is away on holiday. Should do you fine while you work things out." He did a loop at Trafalgar Square and headed back the way he had come, past the Savoy once more. Donny could see the team vehicle outside, and the pair of watchers standing at the junction with the Strand. They did not appear to have been spotted.

***

The boat Charlie mentioned, turned out to be fifty-five foot of converted admiral's barge, with a raised roof to the long saloon. It was fitted in luxury style for two couples, with two single cabins for crew/staff. It was linked to the shore for power and services, though, as Charlie pointed out it was a simple matter to disconnect, and the engines were maintained.

It seemed Charlie's friend knew which way was up and, as an alternative method of escape, justified the cost of its keep. He dropped them off, promising to return with provisions, and left them to explore.

On the other side of the river to the left, downriver, the Millennium Dome, now called the O2, stood, and just upriver Canary Wharf dominated the skyline. The boat moved lazily to the rhythm of the occasional passing river boat.

Settling in, the four rapidly removed their various disguises. When Charlie returned he was shocked to see how young they all were. "What's this all about then, the dressing-up and all that?"

"We're on the run, actually." Abby said. "M16 and the CIA are after us."

"Pull the other one, girl. I wasn't born yesterday. Why would they be interested in you lot? Why, I'm older than all of you, and I've only just come off the bottle."

Donny pulled out his wallet. The warrant card was complete with photograph and proper stamps. Charlie looked at it then at the other three. "I guessed you had to be kosher, otherwise Antoine would not have brought me in." He shook his head and raised his hands. "He's not worried about me. It's his daughter, my wife, he worries about. Between us we get on fine. I don't hire out to hooky geezers. That's villains to you. I keep straight. He keeps happy, and he sends me plenty of business from the hotel. So we all profit. Right. So what do you want to do about the CIA and M16?"

"Oh, we'll handle it, Charlie. We did not expect you to get involved." Donny hastened to say.

"Well, since I'm already involved, bringing you here and that, what do you want to do next? I do have resources hereabouts."

"Resources?"

"Mates. I was brought up round here. You need mates to survive. They look after each other. Mates of my mates get looked after, too, if you take my meaning. It's a point of honour round here."

"I see," Donny said thoughtfully. "Well, it would be good to know if any one starts sniffing about."

"That will happen anyway. I'm talking about positive things we can do."

"We would have to think about that, Charlie. The guys we are dealing with come tooled-up and mob-handed."

"Sounds like fun. My lads will be about if you need us. I'll see they don't step in too soon or anything." Charlie was quite serious about it.

Donny looked at Tom, who grinned, "Sounds good to me, Charlie. I'll keep you in the loop."

The group of four decided that the situation was not really amenable to positive action. They were not yet aware of the forces against them. While the CIA could not be trusted, Donny's friend in the FBI informed him that they were not on the FBI wanted list. This implied that they were not even on the CIA official wanted list.

Importantly they were also not on M15/6 lists. So at the British end at least the opposition was hired-in private only. The possibility was that the US end was also mainly private. There had to be limits to any activities against a friendly nation's security services. Too much pressure and the red flags would go up. Investigations would be undertaken.

Donny called Charlie on his codex cell phone.

"Charlie," the voice answered, "Who wants me?"

The codex gave no information forward, nor was it detectable on the normal network.

"Charlie, its Donny Weston. I think our problem has been handed to private contractors. If your friends have any ideas, like who or where? I am not asking for protection, just information."

Charlie at the other end of the phone said, "I've got the idea. Leave it with me. I'll be in touch during the next couple of hours."

The weather managed to perform its own minor miracle. The four friends were soon strewn about on the afterdeck of the boat in comfortable chairs discussing forthcoming cruises in the Mediterranean.

When the codex rang Donny picked it up. "It's Charlie, Do you know someone called Remington?"

"Big fellow, American hunk, according to the girls!"

"That's the one. He arrived at the airport in London an hour ago. He went direct to the Savoy. Antoine has him in sight and my pal is on tap to drive him about. Should we worry?"

Donny thought for a moment. "He is our problem. He is lethal and he wants us terminated. I guess he will be in touch with the contractors. He is unlikely to undertake wet work himself, but is quite willing to watch it done!"

"I'll warn the lads. Mustn't allow things to get out of hand, must w? Need anything?"

"We could do with a change of clothes. Is there anywhere around here that can supply?"

"Take the tender and cross the river to Greenwich. The town there has at all, plus pretty good restaurants. I don't need to tell you to watch out when you return. It pays to be careful."

"Right, Charlie. Message received. Thanks for the info and keep us posted if you can."

"Will do. Bye." Charlie rang off.

All four crossed the river in the launch moored alongside the houseboat. The keys had been hanging in the cabinet along with the main engine keys for the barge. Curiosity had driven Tom to have a look into the engine room. His comment was interesting. "I expected to see a single diesel, perhaps the original wing engine for the boat. What I found was a pair of high power, Mercedes turbo-diesel engines. This craft must do at least 40-45 knots. But I noticed there was a diagram on the bulkhead. The engines will run driving traditional props through the inboard-outboard fittings. If you lean over the stern you can see them. But in fact the power can be diverted, by raising the outboard drives. The power is channelled through two water-jet systems to produce way more power. Raising the outboards cleans up the bottom. My guess would be 60 knots at least, maybe more."

"Wow. It makes you wonder what business the owner carried on." Donny smiled, "Having said that, 'be thankful for small mercies' as my mother used to say. Let's go to Greenwich."

The visit was productive, though it was diffi-cult to prize the two girls away from the collection of small shops where, in their words, 'interesting things' were available.

They fed in an Italian restaurant with a window overlooking the passing pageant of river traffic.

Their table was not in close proximity to any other and Donny leaned forward to speak to the others. "Playtime is over, folks. I hope you enjoyed it. The presence of Remington in London means serious trouble if he is allowed to get away with it. Madam Fitch may not have us on a shoot on sight list, but I bet we are on a find and report list.

"That would be all Remington needs. Once we are spotted, keeping tracks on us is not so difficult. What I plan is that we go and see the man and see if there is a way out of this mess.

The three appalled faces made him laugh. "Kidding, I wanted to see if you were actually lis-tening, or perhaps still contemplating a bargain you found in a shop in the High street."

He sat back. "Ideas?"

***

The trip back to the barge was complicated by the darkness that had fallen and the minor inconven-ience of not leaving a light on. They solved the problem by putting Donny ashore at the steps, and waiting until he called from the boat to let them know where it was actually moored. There was a lot of chiff-chaff back and forth about sailors and navigation, but when all were aboard the atmosphere became very serious.

Donny pointed out that there had been an attempt to break into the boat while they were away. The next boat along was occupied by a bodybuilder, who saw the person snooping about. He had confronted the intruder, who had taken off at high speed. The man had not got into the boat, but the question was there. Was it a thief, or was it one of the Remington people?

They decided to set up a watch system through the night, based on watches at sea. They managed to survive the night with no further alarms.

***

Peter Speight eased the *Stroller* into the berth at St Katherine's dock. The entire marina there was packed full of boats which he guessed never moved from one year's end, to the other. Probably £3 million pounds worth, in smaller boats, the bigger ones were more like that figure each. He grinned. *Stroller* at least could claim to have sea time. He had just brought her down from Leith. She had waited there while his arm recovered. It was just about okay now, though he still favoured it where he could.

The man standing on the quay as he came alongside, took the mooring ropes as he handed them out, and secured the boat to the dock.

Peter was not really fond of Remington, but he had contracted to the CIA for work and he was stuck with it. The last episode was upsetting. He discovered his daughter had been sleeping with the man. While he was not a prude he did recognise that the man was dangerous. When he had received the call for this job he had really thought twice about it. But the up-front money and the payment for the repairs persuaded him.

***

Remington stood tall and remote in the window of his apartment in the Tower Hotel. He was watching the bridge closing, having opened to let a vessel through. "That doesn't happen very often now," he said. "I'm glad I have seen it for myself." He turned to Peter Speight. "How is the arm? Fully recovered I hope. Was it all paid for properly?"

"It was, and the damage to the boat, thank you." Peter spoke clearly and a little louder than he would have to an English person. He still suffered from the habit generated in his youth of shouting at the foreigners in the Arcade when they didn't understand him.

In his softer voice, Remington said, "My local people reckon that the target has gone to ground, 'so to speak', in a boat."

"Here, on the Thames?" Peter asked.

"Yes. It seems they were seen with a known fixer, in the area who uses a boat moored alongside the Isle of Dogs in the Thames to keep people out of sight. We think that is where the targets are and we need to find them and eliminate them."

"Is there a reason for this, ah, elimination?"

"That is no concern of yours. Enough to say that M16 is fully aware of the situation and is giving their cooperation."

"I see, and you want me to find these people in their boat along the moorings at the Isle of Dogs?"

"That is the case in a nutshell."

"You do not want me to shoot them?"

"No. I do not want you to shoot them."

"If they shoot at me, can I shoot back?"

"Just find the boat. We will do the rest."

Peter Speight smiled as he left the hotel. It occurred to him that Remington had not told him not to contact these targets.

The idea was wandering about in his mind as he waited for the lock gates to open to release his boat from the marina. Remington had not taken this particular element into his calculations. Time, as he had always said, was a prime consideration. He wondered where his daughter, Natalie, was, as he

threaded his way between two tugs passing in opposite directions in the tideway. He was fond of his
daughter in his own sort of way. As Wapping slid
by he slid on at a stately five knots round the sharp
right hand bend, past Rotherhithe on the south side
and Millwall on the left. This was the Isle of Dogs
and he now needed to keep his eyes well open, if he
was to get away with what he had come up with.

His third stooge past the moorings got results.
On the deck of the converted admiral's barge which
he had admired on his previous two passes, stood
Lotte, the girl he remembered from Inverbervie.
The girl on the schooner, *Speedwel*.

"Hullo!" He said. "Fancy meeting you here."
He throttled back until he was just stemming the
current.

"Do you happen to know a man called Remington, a big chap, American CIA and all that."

"Yes, I do. Why? Do you know him, too?"

"He asked me to locate you and your three
friends. I have the impression he doesn't like you."

"You are probably right. What are you going to
do?"

"I shall probably tell him where you are. After
all, he is paying me to do that. I will not tell him
that we have talked. So, unless he has a man on the
shore watching us, he won't know.

"If I am found out, I will tell him that I was passing the time, chatting up a pretty girl on the water. It is after all, what we boat people do, is it not?"

Lotte grinned, "Thank you, kind sir. I will try and miss you, if we start shooting at each other."

"And I also. You may tell your friends, all others are fair game."

The passing boat speeded up. Peter Speight picked up his cell and reported that the quarry had been located.

***

For Paul Remington, this operation had been lengthy and time-consuming, commencing with the initial planning, and the retrieval of the information carried by Commander Pleasance. The debacle in France over the contractors, plus the ham-fisted, so-called assistance of the UK security people, and finally the incredible disaster of the assassination, or should he say the non-assassination. The final cut had been the desertion of Natalie when he needed her.

Acknowledging that the result so far had been to his career advantage did not really mend matters. He would never forgive those interfering rogue M16 agents for preventing him from carrying out the scheme which would have distanced his country from Europe. His former chief had seen the purpose behind the operation and had taken the fall for its failure. He shrugged. That was life. Reaping the benefit gave him the chance to remove the group which had dogged his footsteps for the entire time he had been in Europe. Now he knew where they were, he would personally do the job that the others should have done.

***

Lotte Compton watched Peter Speight move upriver. The clean lines of the *Stroller* made easy work against the current. She opened her cell phone and called Tom. Detailing the conversation, she suggested that the assault would probably be two-handed; by land and by river. She also suggested that the team reassemble pronto, as she did not have enough firepower on her own.

"We will be with you in 30 minutes," Tom said. "Charlie was just arranging for some odds and ends to reinforce our armoury."

***

The limo turned up 27 minutes later. All three of the others poured out, laden with bags and bundles. They dumped them on board and Tom jumped into the tender to detach it from its connections to the barge.

Charlie disconnected the shore services, then went to the mooring ropes and unloosed all but the bow and stern spring lines. The boat started to move snubbing against the looser mooring. The engines started to burble. With Abby at the helm, Donny called Charlie to loosen the bow rope, and push the boat off. The bow, caught by the current began to swing out from the shore, still held by the stern rope, Abby touched the throttle. As the boat moved forward toward mid-river, the stern cleared the quay wall. Charlie, hauling the stern line allowed the boat to pivot, turning it end to end, until it was facing downriver. Then Abby reversed the engines and, guided from the shore by Charlie, the boat was brought alongside once more. In the same place, but facing downriver to the North Sea.

They had worked it out on the way back. Rather than face attack from two directions they would force the attackers to meet on more equal terms, on the water as before, though the waters were a little more confined this time.

Donny sent Charlie to connect with his mates up river to keep an eye out for Peter Speight's boat, or any other boat the opposition might use.

"Lotte, here is an Uzi, there are three magazines here. Can you handle it?"

Lotte grinned. "Piece of cake," she said, checking the action and slotting in the first magazine and setting the safety.

To Abby went the Armalite-ar15, with two 20-shot magazines.

Tom took the under-and-over. Firing grenades out of the lower barrel, it fires 7.65mm semi-automatic bullets from the upper. The 32-shot magazine was attached already and a tube of grenades was available to reload the grenade launcher.

Donny kept the H&K smg to himself. All had their automatics.

"Well, that seems to be it for now. Let's eat." Donny turned to the others, "It's been fun! And just in case, I wouldn't have missed it for the world."

"We'll talk about it when we celebrate tomorrow." Abby repeated. "Let's eat."

***

The warning came in the late afternoon. The *Stroller* was coming downriver and there were several people aboard. The group all knew what to do. They swung into action. The moorings were loosed and cast off. The engines rumbled into action.

"Has anyone asked the owner if we can take his boat to sea?" Tom asked.

"Probably not. It might worry him." Abby answered.

"That's what insurance is for." Lotte called.

Donny said, "That presumes it is insured. I would not be surprised if it wasn't."

Charlie's voice came up from below, surprising them all. They had not realised he was there. "It's insured. The insurance people don't know the owner is abroad. As long as it's lived in, the insurance is in force."

"What the devil are you doing here, Charlie?" Donny was annoyed.

"You've gotta be kidding." He appeared carrying a double-barrelled, over-and-under gun.

"What on earth is that?" Donny asked gazing in bewilderment at the enormous gun.

"This is a Webley & Scott, special edition elephant gun. Bored to fire a .40 solid-jacketed round from the rifle, and 12 bore solid round from the lower barrel. He produced a bag of bullets of both calibres. "My dad brought this back from India, after the war. I always swore it would come in useful one day."

"Have you ever fired it?" Abby asked interestedly.

"Nah. How difficult can it be?" Charlie said, a little less confidently. "Now's me chance to make a difference."

They were motoring down the river now, the *Stroller* in sight behind them. They were approaching Gravesend. They increased speed, gradually pulling away, extending their lead.

"What is the name of this boat? Abby was on the cabin roof stretched out behind a barrier of boat fenders. Charlie answered, "It is called the '*Dream.*' The silly sod who owns it said he would sail off one day and live on it for the rest of his days. So what does he do when he gets the chance? He buggered off with a posh totty, who wouldn't go in the boat because, when she had visited him here, she slipped and broke a nail."

Abby looked over the cabin roof at him.

Charlie blushed. "Well it was some silly reason, I know that. That left me with the boat. I often come down to it for a bit of peace and quiet."

The shot was a surprise. The pursuing boat had caught up a bit.

Donny opened the throttle and the stern dug in. The river was wider now with the long pier of Southend ahead on the port bow.

"Right. Let's see what they have got," said Donny. He opened the throttles wide and let the '*Dream*' go. The stern dug in deep and the bow rose. The wake widened and the speed dial on the dashboard, crept up to 35, then 40 knots. The other boat responded and began to catch them up.

Donny called to Abby. "Discourage them a little. It's too public to sink them here."

The crack of the shots was difficult to hear over the roar of the engines. Tom, who was watching the other craft, yelled, "That's a new windscreen, they'll need."

"Let me have a go," Charlie offered. He settled down and sighted through the telescopic sight. The noise of the elephant gun was very loud and, de-

scribed by Lotte later as somewhere between Vesu-
vius and atom bomb.

"You've chopped off her radar mast," Tom
said delightedly.

"Broken my bloody shoulder, more like," said
Charlie ruefully, rubbing the bruised area vigor-
ously.

A spray of bullets suddenly disturbed the already turbulent water around them. Two or three hit
the boat sinking into the wood. From the roof of the
cabin, Abby fired a series of shots. One of the men
on deck toppled into the water. Another volley
came from the followers, the bullets whistling
around the *Dream* without hitting anyone. The estuary was opening wide ahead of the two speeding
boats. Southend Pier was way behind, still in view
but now miles away.

"Right. Get it together, people. I'm going to
come about and take the war to them. Are you
ready?" Donny was poised to put the wheel over.

All four called that they were ready. Charlie
loaded the 12 bore. There was a full magazine in the
.40 cal. He lay with a pad wedged into his jacket at
the shoulder, rifle across the starboard side of the
cockpit. He opened proceedings when the *Stroller*
came into his view, firing the 12 bore for the first
time. With the range closing fast, his shot hit the
bow. The effect was devastating. The joint, where
the deck and the two sides met, disintegrated at the

impact. The stem began to separate under the batter-
ing from the speed through the water. Charlie
ducked below the bulwarks, as bullets smashed in to
the swiftly closing boat. Abby was firing a steady
stream of bullets at the other craft. Three of the
visible men on deck were down. The tall figure of
Remington was standing beside the crouched figure
of Pater Speight who was driving the boat. The carbine Remington was using was spouting bullets, but
with little effect. Charlie rose above the bulwark.
Lining the rifle up, he squeezed the trigger. Then he
dropped to the deck swearing. Blood appeared on
his jacket shoulder. On the other boat Remington
had been thrown backward across the after cabin
roof. Sliding and slipping he was weakly trying to
stop himself from falling into the water boiling past
the port side of the boat. Peter Speight left the
wheel, to try and grab him, but too late. Remington
went, bleeding badly from his shattered chest, into
the turmoil of the tidal waters. He sank and was lost
in the wake of the racing boat. At the wheel Peter
Speight throttled back.

Donny called to his crew to cease fire. "Lotte,
see to Charlie. He has been hit."

Abby came off the roof. Tom, who had not
fired a shot, came through to lend a hand.

Donny came alongside the now stopped
Stroller. Peter Speight was trying to help the two

surviving men, both wounded. Abby jumped over to give a hand. "Where is Remington?" She asked .

Peter shrugged. "Stupid sod stood shooting his carbine. He didn't hit anything that I could see, but he had to be the biggest target. Whatever that cannon was that shot him blew him apart. He went over the side before I could catch him. He is back there somewhere. But I'll guarantee he's dead, that's for sure.

The two wounded still on board would both survive.

As Abby went to return to the *Dream* she turned to Peter. "This is over. Thanks for the warning by the way."

Peter smiled wryly. "At least you were willing to listen. The boat's a mess, but I've been well paid for her. If you could give me," he shrugged, indicating the two wounded, "us a lift, I think the *Stroller* had had its day."

Abby looked at the sinking foredeck. "I think we probably should."

Tom. Donny and Peter helped the wounded men over into *Dream* and then let Tom fire his unused grenade launcher at the stern of the other boat. Now open to the sea at her heaviest point the *Stroller* sank finally to the bottom.

Nothing was reported, or said, about the battle in the Thames estuary.

***

The disappearance of Paul Remington was re-marked within the walls of the CIA headquarters in Langley. Officially he had not come to England and therefore did not exist on this side of the Atlantic.

***

Jonathon returned from his assignment abroad.

Calling on Donny and Abby, he asked how the other pair, Tom and Lotte, were settling in.

"Fine," said Abby. "We have seen a lot of them while you have been away. We decided not to re-port in to HQ until you returned. We were a little unsure of Madam Fitch's reception.

"Is there anything you should be telling me about? Did anything happen while I was away?"

Both Donny and Abby replied, "Nothing, as far as we are concerned."

The End

Meet our author

David O'Neil

Artist and Photographer David O'Neil started writing seriously with a series of Highland guide books. His boyhood
ambitions were to fly an aeroplane, and sail a boat. As a boy
he and his family were bombed out of their home in London.
He learned to fly with the RAF during his National Service. He
started sailing boats while serving in the Colonial Police, in
Nyasaland (Malawi). He spent 8 years there, before returning
to UK. Since then he lived in southern England where he became a management consultant, for over twenty years. He
returned to live in Scotland in 1980, and became a tour guide
in1986. He started writing in 2006, the first guide book being
published in 2007. A further two have been published since
He started writing fiction in 2007 and has now written eleven
full length novels. He has a collection of short stories in publi-
cation at present.

Also by David O'Neil

Exciting, Isn't It?

O'Neil's initial entry into the world of action adventure romance thriller is filled with mystery and suspense, thrills and chills as *Counterstroke* finds it seeds of Genesis, and springs full blown onto the scene with action, adventure and romance galore.

John Murray, ex-Police, ex-MI6, ex management consultant, 49 and widowed, is ready to make a new start. Having sold off everything, he sets out on a lazy journey by barge through the waterways of France to collect his yacht at a yard in Grasse. En route he will decide what to do with the rest of his life

He picks up a female hitch-hiker Gabrielle, a frustrated author running from Paris after a confrontation with a lascivious would-be publisher Mathieu. She had unknowingly picked up some of Mathieu's secret documents with her manuscript. Although not looking for action, adventure or romance, still a connection is made.

An encounter with Pierre, an unpleasant former acquaintance from Paris who is chasing Gabrielle, is followed by a series of events that make John call on all his old skills of survival to keep them both alive over the next few days. Mystery and suspense shroud the secret documents that disclose the real background of the so called publisher who is in fact a high level international crook.

To survive, the pair become convinced they must take the fight to the enemy but they have no illusions; their chances of survival are slim. But with the help of some of John's old contacts, things start to become... exciting.

Counterstroke # 2....

Market Forces

Market Forces, Volume Two of the Counterstroke action adventure romance thriller series by David O'Neil introduces Katherine (Katt) Percival, tasked with the assassination of Mark Parnell in a hurried, last-minute attempt to stop his interference with the success of the Organization in Europe. As a skilled terminator for the CIA, Katt is accustomed to proper briefing. On this occasion she disobeys her orders, convinced it's a mistake. She joins forces with Mark to foil an attempt on his life.

Parnell works for John Murray, who created Secure Inc that caused the collapse of an International US criminal organisation's operation in Europe, forcing the disbanding of the US Company COMCO. Set up as a cover for money-laundering and other operations designed to control from within the political and financial administration, they had already been partially successful. Especially within the administrative sectors of the EU.

Katt goes on the run, she has been targeted and her Director sidelined by rogue interests in the CIA. She finds proof of conspiracy. She passes it on to Secure Inc who can use it to attack the Organization. She joins forces with Mark Parnell and Secure Inc. Mark and Katt and their colleagues risk their lives as they set out to foil the Organization once again.

Counterstroke # 3....

When Needs Must...

The latest action adventure thriller in the Counterstroke series opens with a new character Major Teddy Robertson–Steel fighting for survival in Africa. Mark Parnell and Katt Percival now working together for Secure Inc. are joined by Captain Libby 'Carter' Barr, now in plain clothes, well mostly, and her new partner James Wallace. They are tasked with locating and thwarting the efforts of three separate menaces from the European scene that threaten the separation of the United Kingdom from the political clutches of Brussels, by using terrorism to create wealth by a group of billionaires, and the continuing presence of the Mob, bankrolled from USA. An action adventure thriller filled with romance, mystery and suspense. With the appearance of a much needed new team, Dan and Reba, and the welcome return of Peter Maddox, Dublo Bond and Tiny Lewis, there is action and adventure throughout. Change will happen, it just takes the right people, at the right time, in the right place.

Young adult action/adventure/ romance thriller series
Donny Weston & Abby Marshall # 1

Fatal Meeting
A captivating new series of young adult action, romance, adventure and mystery.

For two young teens, Donny and Abby, who have just found each other, sailing the 40 ft ketch across the English Channel to Cherbourg is supposed to be a light-hearted adventure.

The third member of the crew turns out to be a smuggler, and he attempts to kill them both before they reach France. The romance adventure. now filled with action, mystery and suspense, suddenly becomes deadly serious when the man's employers try to recover smuggled items from the boat. The action gets more and more hectic as the motive becomes personal

Donny and Abby are plunged into a series of events that force them to protect themselves. Donny's parents become involved so with the help of a friend of the family, Jonathon Glynn, they take the offensive against the gang who are trying to kill them.

The action adventure thriller ranges from the Mediterranean to Paris and the final scene is played out in the shadow of the Eiffel Tower in the city of romance and lights; Paris France..

Donny Weston & Abby Marshall # 2

Lethal Complications

Eighteen year olds Donny and Abby take a year out from their studies to clear up problems that had escalated over the past three years. They succeed in closing the book on the past during the first months of the year, now they are looking forward to nine months relaxation, romance and fun, when old friend of the family, mystery man Jonathon Glynn, drops in to visit as they moor at Boulogne, bringing action and adventure into their lives once again.

Jonathon was followed and an attempt to kill them happens immediately after his visit. They leave their boat and
pick up the RV they have left in France, hoping to avoid further conflict. They are attacked in the Camargue, but fast and
accurate shooting keeps them alive. They find themselves
mixed up in a treacherous scheme by a rogue Chinese gang to
defame a Chinese moderate, in an attempt to stall the Democratic process in China.

The two young lovers, becoming addicted to action and
adventure, link up with Isobel, a person of mystery who has
acquired a reputation without earning it. Between them they
manage to keep the Chinese target and his girlfriend out of
the rogue Chinese group's hands.

Tired of reacting to attack, and now looking for action
and adventure, they set up an ambush of their own, effec-
tively checkmating the rogue Chinese plans. The leader of the
rogues, having lost face and position in the Chinese hierarchy,
plans a personal coup using former Spetsnaz mercenaries.
With the help of a former SBS man Adam, who had worked
with and against Spetsnaz forces, the friends survive and Lin
Hang the Chinese leader suffers defeat.

Donny Weston & Abby Marshall # 3....

A Thrill A Minute

They are back! Fresh from their drama-filled action adventure excursion to the United States, Abby Marshall and
Donny Weston look forward to once again taking up their
studies at the University. Each of them is looking forward to
the calm life of a University student without the threat of
being murdered. Ah, the serene life.... that is the thing. But
that doesn't last long. It is only a few weeks before our ad-

venturesome young lovers find that the calm, quiet routine of University life is boring beyond belief and both are filled with yearning for the fast-paced action adventure of their prior experiences. It isn't long before trouble finds the couple and they welcome it with open arms, but perhaps this time they have underestimated the opposition. Feeling excitement once again, the two youths arm themselves and leapt into the fray. The fight was on and no holds barred!

Once again O'Neil takes us into the action filled world of mystery and suspense, action and adventure, romance and peril.

Donny Weston & Abby Marshall # 4....

It's Just One Thing After Another

Fresh from their victory over the European Mafia, our two young adults in love, Abby Marshall and Donny Weston, are rewarded with an all-expense-paid trip to the United States. But, as our young couple discover, there is no free lunch and the price they will have to pay for their "free" tour may be more than they can afford to pay, in this action adventure thriller. Even so, with the help of a few friends and some former enemies, the valiant young duo face danger once again with firm resolve and iron spirit, but will that be sufficient in face of the odds that are stacked against them?

And is their friend and benefactor actually a friend or is he on the other side? The two young adults look at this man of mystery and suspense with a bit of caution. Action, adventure and romance abound in this, the latest escapades of Britain's dynamic young couple.

Donny Weston & Abby Marshall # 5

What Goes Around...

Just when it seems that our two young heroes, Donny Weston and Abby Marshall are able to return to the University to complete their studies, fate decides to play another turn as once again the two young lovers come under attack, this time from a most unsuspected source. It appears that not even the majestic powers of the British Intelligence Service will be enough to rescue the beleaguered duo and they will have to survive through their own skills. In the continuing action adventure thriller, two young adults must solve the mystery that faces them to determine who is trying to kill them. The suspense is chilling, the action and adventure stimulating. Finding togetherness even among the onslaughts, Donny and Abby also find remarkable friends who offer their assistance; but will even that be enough to overcome the determined enemy?

Donny Weston & Abby Marshall # 6

Without Prejudice

Donny Weston and Abby Marshall, on their way to park their beloved boat *Swallow* in Malta to be ready for the summer, encounter the schooner *Speedwell* at La Rochelle, where problems arise for Commander Will and his wife Mary Pleasance. Tom Hardy and Lotte Compton, both from the *Speedwell* join forces with Donny and Abby to oppose the threats to the Commander. From Valetta the four follow up the threat, only to find themselves faced with a plot to use a famous mercenary in an assassination that will rock the foundations of the Euro community, and the western world. Backed by Russia and with the tacit approval of the head of MI6, a rogue CIA operative has set things up for a public shooting at a Euro summit.

The four foil the plot and the assassination fails, but ironically the CIA agent, is credited with foiling the coup and promoted. He wants revenge, and comes after the four with blood in his eye and his guns loaded. The outcome is decided in a action-packed shoot-out in high speed boats in the cold waters of the Thames estuary.

Sea Adventures

Better The Day

From the W.E.B. Griffin of the United Kingdom, David O'Neil, a exciting saga of romance, action, adventure, mystery and suspense as Peter Murray and his brother officers in Coastal Forces face overwhelming odds fighting German E-boats, the German Navy and the Luftwaffe in action in the Channel, the Mediterranean, Norway and the Baltic – where there is conflict with the Soviet Allies. This action-packed story of daring and adventure finally follows Peter Murray to the Pacific where he faces Kamikaze action with the U.S. Fleet.

Distant Gunfire

"Border s Away!" Serving as an officer on a British frigate at the time of the French Emperor Napoleon is not the safest occupation, but could be a most profitable one. Robert

Graham, rising from the ranks to become the Captain of a British battleship by virtue of his dauntless leadership, displayed under enemy fire, finds himself a wealthy man as the capture of enemy ships resulted in rich rewards. Action and adventure is the word of the day, as battle after battle rages across the turbulent waters and seas as the valiant British Royal Navy fights to stem the onslaught of the mighty French Army and Navy. Mystery and suspense abound as inserting and collecting spy agent after spy agent is executed. The threat of imminent death makes romance and romantic interludes all the sweeter, and the suspense of waiting for a love one to return even more traumatic. Captain Graham, with his loyal following of sailors and marines, takes prize ship after prize ship, thwart plot after diabolical plot, and finds romance when he least expects it. To his amazement and joy, he finds himself being knighted by the King of England. The good life is his, now all he has to do is to live long enough to enjoy it. A rollicking good tale of sea action and swashbuckling adventures.

Sailing Orders

For those awaiting another naval story of the 18/19th century, then this is it. Following the life of an abandoned 13 year old who by chance is instrumental in saving a family from robbery and worse. Taken in by the naval Captain Bowers he is placed as a midshipman in his benefactor's ship. From that time onward with the increasing demands of the conflict with France, Martin Forrest grows up fast. The relationship with his benefactors family is formalised when he is adopted by them and has a home once more. Romance with Jennifer the Captains ward links him ever closer to the family.

Meanwhile he serves in the West Indies where good fortune results in his gaining considerable wealth personally. With promotion and command he is able to marry and reclaim his birth-right, stolen from him by his step-mother and her lover.

The mysterious (call me merely Mr Smith) involves Martin in more activity in the shadowy world of the secret agents. Mainly a question of lifting and placing of people, his involvement becomes more complex as time goes on. A cruise to India consolidates his position and rank with the successful capture of prizes when returning convoying East-Indiamen. His rise to Post rank is followed by a series of events, that sadly culminate in family tragedy.

While still young Martin Forrest-Bowers faces and empty future, though merely Mr Smith has requested his services????

Adventure thrillers

Minding the Store

O'Neil scores again! Often favourably compared to America's W.E.B. Griffin and to U.K.'s Ian Fleming, and fresh from his best-selling action adventure, "Distant Gunfire," O'Neil finds excitement and action in the New York garment district. The department store industry becomes the target of take-over by organized crime in their quest for money-laundering outlets. It would seem that no department store executive is a match for vicious criminals, however, David Freemantle, heir to the Freemantle fortune and Managing Director of America's most prestigious department store is no ordinary department store executive and the team of ex-military specialists he has assembled contains no ordinary store security personnel. Armed invasions are met with swift retaliation; kidnapping and rape attempts are met with fatal consequences as the Mafia and their foreign cohorts learn that not all ordinary citizens are helpless, and that evil force can be met with superior force in O'Neil's latest thriller of adventure and action, romance and suspense, mystery and mayhem that will have the reader on the edge of his seat until the last breath-taking word.

The Hunted

David O'Neal, UK's answer to W.E.B. Griffin and Dean Koontz strikes again with his newest suspense thriller filled with action, adventure, romance and danger. When the Russian Mafia joins forces with other European and Asian gangsters to take over a noted world-wide charity organization to smuggle guns and drugs into unsuspecting nations and begins to kill innocent people, one man – Tarquin Gilmore – Quin to his friends – declares war on the Mafia. To achieve his goal of total destruction of the criminal gangs, he surrounds himself with a few dangerous men and beautiful women. But don't be fooled by their beauty, the girls are easily as deadly as any man. On the other hand, there are a lot more gangsters than Quin and his friends and it's a battle to the finish. A stirring tale of crime and murder, mystery and suspense, passion and romance, guns and drugs... but that is war!

The Mercy Run

O'Neil's thrilling action adventure saga of Africa: the story of Tom Merrick, Charlie Hammond and Brenda Cox; a man and two women who fight and risk their lives to keep supplies rolling into the U.N. refugee camps in Ethiopia. Their adversaries: the scorching heat, the dirt roads and the ever present hazards of bandit gangs and corrupt government officials. Despite tragedy and treachery, mystery and suspense while combating the efforts of Colonel Gonbera, who hopes to turn the province into his personal domain, Merrick and his friends manage to block the diabolical Colonel at every turn.

Frustrated by Merrick's success against him, there seems to be no depths to which the Colonel would not descend to achieve his aim. The prospect of a lucrative diamond strike comes into the game, and so do the Russians and Chinese. But, as Merrick knows, there will be no peace while the Colonel remains the greatest threat to success and peace.

*****

Available from:

WEB Publishers Inc
www.a-argusbooks.com